Checkmate

Danielle Bolcar

Pen & Pad Publishing LLC

Checkmate
Copyright © 2016 by Danielle Bolcar

Cover design by Dillon Powell.

Printed in the United States of America

ISBN 978-0-9972837-0-9

Pen & Pad Publishing LLC
http://www.penpadpublishing.com   /PenPadPublishingLLC
jasmin@penpadpublishing.com   /penpadpublish

Other Books From
Pen & Pad Publishing LLC

Barrel Child by Pamela K. Marshall

Breaking The Cycle: A Barrel Child Story
by Pamela K. Marshall

The Men I Let Define Love by Janelle Williams

Children Are Like Cupcakes by Ansaba Gavor

Dedication

I would like to dedicate this book to my son.
He was the motivation.
I'd also like to dedicate this to the one who got away.
He was the inspiration.

Definition of ENDGAME

/ 'en(d)-,gām/

noun

1. Chess: The stage of the game when few pieces are left on the board; the king plays an important role during this stage of the game as it can act as a strong attacking piece

2. The final stage of an extended process or course of events

"If you want to win at chess, begin with the ending."
— Irving Chernev (1900-1981), chess player and prolific Russian-American chess author

CHAPTER ONE

Lloyd

He gave me back my self-confidence. Some feminists might want to throttle me for making such a statement, but from the very beginning, he not only drew me in but raised me up. He made me feel like I could do and *be* more. I was not just the small-town Florida girl who got knocked up at nineteen, and who no one really thought would amount to much. In his eyes, I was Leann – super mom, super girlfriend, super woman.

He knew what my ex-boyfriend had put me through and did everything in his power to make sure that I never again felt powerless and expendable. He would often tell me how brave and strong I was to have made it to the other side – no longer a pawn, but now a queen. More importantly, I was the queen to his king. I teased him mercilessly when he would get wrapped up in his chess metaphors, pontificating about the fate of man, war, and even love. But I secretly adored that he could be so passionate and profound.

I did not hesitate when he suggested we do something impulsive. I trusted him completely. He was my endgame. No matter what life threw at us, I was sure that he and I would be standing together at the end. So here we sat, in a Manhattan tattoo parlor, waiting to get matching king and queen chess pieces tattooed on our wrists. Now we would have a piece of each other

1

forever.

♟

Eight years later…

My eyes pulsated as I stared at the clock. I wanted out. Not just out from behind this desk or out of the building for the day, but out of this job and its mind-numbing mediocrity.

"Did you fill out the paperwork for tomorrow's meeting, Leann?" said my boss.

"No, sorry. I'll get right on it."

The little hands of the clock moved slower as I picked up a pen and mindlessly filled out one piece of paperwork after another. My thoughts were desperately trying to flee the remedial work I had been tasked with.

There had to be something more exhilarating than being a nursing home receptionist that I could devote forty hours to each week. Maybe I could be the person that removed the air from a light bulb and lined it with filament. Surely that would be more exciting than this job.

It was ten minutes until four when I realized I was counting the seconds in each minute on the black and white clock hanging on the wall. No calls had come in for the past twenty minutes, and no one had entered or left the building in over an hour. I glanced at the stack of files on my desk that needed to be put in alphabetical order. At least the menial task would help me pass the time.

Paperwork done. Files all alphabetized and stored away. And there were still fifteen minutes left to toil away behind this desk.

That's when he walked in.

But it wasn't the right *he*; it was just the UPS guy. His presence would not have affected me so much if it had not been for that minty-vanilla scent. I was instantly overwhelmed by the unapologetic smell of Versace's Eros cologne as he approached me. Although he wore a little too much for my taste, the fragrance itself was like an olfactory scrapbook, bringing back a flood of memories and emotions that I had spent a lot of time trying to bury. This was the cologne that belonged to *him*.

It had been three years since that particular scent had wafted past me, and I was caught off guard. The look of bewilderment on my face probably threw the UPS guy for a loop.

"Ma'am, if you could just sign here," he said, handing me a pen and gesturing to his clipboard. He was in a hurry, probably as anxious as I was to get to the end of this day.

I scribbled my name and that should have been it, but the UPS guy just stood there, glancing from the clipboard to me with a quizzical expression on his face.

Was there something in my teeth? Had he noticed the leftover eyeliner on my face? It was New Year's Day and a mere nine hours earlier I was waking up beside my best friend, shaking confetti out of my hair, before frantically running to the bathroom to get dressed for work. Could he smell last night's alcohol on my breath? No, that couldn't be it.

"Ma'am, I just wanted to know is that two L's or one?" he said, pointing to my signature.

There it was – a name I tried to forget. Lloyd was back, at least in my thoughts. I had signed his name instead of mine without even realizing it. I obviously did not look like a Lloyd, but the UPS guy let it go after I mumbled, "Two L's."

I spent so much time trying to erase Lloyd from my thoughts, yet he crept back in so effortlessly. Clocking out, I watched my fingers brush each number carefully to make sure I didn't punch in Lloyd's phone number or our anniversary date.

I was not in the right mindset to deal with the subway and its eccentric riders and decided it would be best to hail a cab. On most nights, I enjoyed walking the streets of New York City – the smell of sewage, ambulance sirens blaring, Meredith screaming down from her apartment and flinging objects at her boyfriend's head – who wouldn't enjoy that?

Growing up in Florida, these were scenes I had only dreamt about. I was born in New Jersey, but my parents relocated to the South when I was three. Still, for me, the taste of Northern life never left my palate. It wasn't until the age of thirty that I was able to make the leap from the sandy beaches of the South to the crowded streets of the Big Apple. My son was eleven years old, and after the loss of my mother the previous summer, we were both ready for a change of scenery. Moving to a place that did not hold a memory of her at every corner made it a little easier to get back to normal. New York ran faster than a spine-tailed swift, and the change of pace helped keep our minds occupied.

My mother had always been there for me. She stepped in to help me raise my son when his father proved unreliable and I was crippled with a bout of depression. My son's entrance into the world should have been a joyous time, but soon after his birth, an empty, hollow feeling overwhelmed me. I lost sight of myself and foolishly tried to battle my demons alone. My mother saw through my front though. I felt helpless at times, and the guilt of not being able to handle my son on my own ate away at me. Ending my life crossed my mind, and it was my mother that got me through those moments. I pray that she knew how utterly grateful I was, even though my spoiled nature did not always allow me to show it.

Once I got a handle on the depression, I knew that if I could manage to be just half the woman my mother was, then my son and I would be alright. Mom was a mechanic, a plumber, a baker, a tutor, a philanthropist, and an aesthetician. Maybe I was exaggerating a little, but she had me convinced she could do it all. As I waited for a cab, I caught myself smiling in the tinted window of a beauty shop. I had the privilege of knowing an angel on Earth, and for that I was blessed.

A cab neared, and I dug into my purse to make sure I spotted my wallet. I had an unfortunate habit of being absent-minded and quickly learned that while the cab drivers in New York City were worldly and chatty, they were neither forgiving nor understanding if you could not pay your fare. I, unfortunately, was also very clumsy and managed to trip over my feet while rummaging through my purse.

As I lay sprawled on the ground, having at least found my wallet, I remembered how Lloyd used to call me Urkel due to my clumsy nature. In fact, I literally fell into his arms the first time we met.

♟

I was twenty years old, and my son had just turned one. I had a pretty good handle on my depression by that time, but my mom was still worried about me. So when my besties, Melissa and Shay, invited me to tag along on their trip to Daytona Beach for Spring Break, my mother insisted that I go.

I was hesitant to jump back into the swing of college life. I managed to complete all of my freshman year credits, but took the following year off to focus on raising Lorenzo and getting healthy. While my friends were focused on frat parties, homecoming, and the occasional study session, I was busy with diapers, bottles, and onesies. I did not know if I would still fit in.

I also felt guilty about leaving Lorenzo even though I knew

he was in the best care with my mom. And, honestly, I had not lost all the baby weight yet, so I was a bit self-conscious to hit the beach with all the beautiful twenty-somethings who had not, months before, put on forty pounds to bring a new life into this world. Nonetheless, my mom and friends were persistent, and I found myself at the Palms Resort.

As we entered the hotel, throngs of college kids stood around with their luggage, waiting for their rooms to be ready. I tried to remain inconspicuous in my huge, bug-like shades, still not completely comfortable.

I thought we would have a long wait for our room like the other students as it was still two hours before the official check-in time. But somehow, ten minutes after talking to the hotel clerk, a bell hop was at our side, asking to help us with our bags, before escorting us to our room. I'm sure it had *nothing* to do with the flirtations of my busty friend, Shay. Either way, the excitement from the girls and everyone we were around was starting to rub off on me, and I told myself I would do this vacation right – no worrying, no self-doubt, just carefree *fun*.

Three hours later, Shay had to drag me out of bed. I swear I just put my head down for a second to make sure the bed was comfortable, but I must not have accounted for how tired I was. After all, it had been a full year since I hadn't been woken up in the middle of the night for a feeding, diaper change or, the worst of them all, unexplained bawling that was so loud it could have woken the dead.

Melissa and Shay knew that Lorenzo was a handful, and they let me sleep while they scoped out the bar scene. When they returned with a game plan for the night, however, my reprieve was up. They spackled my face with makeup to cover the bags under my eyes and dressed me in the tightest, skimpiest attire of theirs they could find. Apparently, nothing I had packed was up to their standards. When they finally put a mirror in front of me, I had to admit, I looked *damn* good.

Shay handed me the fake ID they had acquired for me, and I resolved to break free and live a little. As we made our way to the pool bar, a few cat calls boosted my confidence even more. The tequila shots Melissa ordered did the rest. By the time Shay called for body shots, I jumped in without hesitation.

We got a good buzz going and then headed for the strip to grab something to eat. Melissa recommended pizza, but Shay and I gave each other "the look." We were both Italian. We grew up on orange-sized meatballs and homemade sauces that our grandmother's grandmother had passed down. Generic strip pizza constructed of canned sauce and processed cheese was not up to our standard in terms of quality.

We outvoted Melissa and told her we'd prefer Greek food instead. Melissa was very opinionated and not one to back down easily, especially with a few drinks in her. She went on and on about pizza, reminiscent of Bubba's soliloquy about shrimp, until we persuaded her the best way we knew how… with men. After pointing out that the Greek place had outdoor seating and an immaculate view of all the passers-by, she realized it was man meat, not pitas, that we were chasing.

Group after group of inebriated, beach-bodied potentials took their time walking past us. I felt like pieces of bread surrounded by starved seagulls. We were showered with marriage proposals, sexual advances, and one guy even asked Melissa if he could smell her feet. Melissa and Shay egged them on, holding up napkins they'd written numbers on to rate the guys walking by. After a margarita, even I joined in on the rating game.

So many numbers had been exchanged that I lost track. All were stored on my phone as Daytona. Texts were being traded faster than stocks. The three of us were getting images you would not dare show your grandmother. One guy sent me a naked photo of him sprawled out on a racecar bed. Needless to say, I was tipsy enough to be a bit impressed. After all, it wasn't every day I met a guy that had a car, or even a license for that matter. I lived in a small, broke town that was polluted with drug dealers and pill-poppers. GEDs were far more likely than Ph.D.'s in my neck of the woods. And here this man had a plastic Viper. But that image was soon topped by a picture Shay received of a guy holding an arrangement of petunias in front of his package. Why not roses? Why not carnations? For the life of me, I couldn't decipher it. I pondered this for quite some time.

Then, *he* walked by.

Lloyd was a bit understated compared to the loud-mouthed, cocky guys he was with, but was by no means a wallflower. While one of his friends, who had tattoos over most of his caramel skin, was taunting cars that drove past in a looking-for-trouble kind of way, Lloyd was a little more reserved. He was tall, dark, and attractive. He wore a navy blue tank top, khaki shorts, and a straw hat. He had an amazing smile that held my attention right away. My jaw dropped as I watched him saunter toward the restaurant.

6

Melissa pulled me out of my trance, kicking my leg under the table.

"You're drooling," she joked. "Who are you looking at?"

"Um, what, no one," I stammered, regaining my composure.

She gave me a sideways look, but went back to rating random guys without hassling me. I pretended to check messages on my phone and noticed that the guy had not gone into the restaurant. He and his friends were standing a few feet away, talking. Now and then, I'd sneak a peek at his perfect lips curved into a smile. From the corner of my eye, I was pretty sure he was sneaking glances at me as well.

The alcohol was still pumping liquid courage through my veins, so I decided to be a bit less furtive with my glances in his direction, hoping he'd take the hint to come over. I was a little disappointed when he, instead, made his way into the restaurant with the other guys.

If I was going to be bold, now was the time. *Why not*, I thought to myself, downing the rest of my margarita in one gulp. Melissa and Shay had worked their magic on me, and I looked good. I had long dark hair with blonde highlights, sun-kissed skin, brown eyes that lightened when the light caught them, and a nice backside – the one place I didn't mind the few extra baby pounds.

"I'm going to get another margarita from the bar. You guys want anything?" I asked the girls as I stood up.

"I'm still working on mine," Melissa said.

"How about another round of shots?" Shay chimed in.

"Ok, I'll be back with shots," I said and headed inside the restaurant.

I kept my eyes peeled for Mr. Dark-and-Handsome as I walked to the bar. I saw some of the guys he had been with at a table, but he was not with them. I took my time, assuming he'd went to the restroom, and hoped he'd return to the table before I started to look like a stalker. I grabbed an open seat at the bar and pretended to be skimming through the drink specials. After five minutes, I started to feel silly. I had not thought this through. Even if I did see him, what was I going to do? Just walk up to his table in front of all his friends and ask for his number? The tequila had not provided *that* much courage.

"Can I get a strawberry margarita, and three shots of Patron?" I told the bartender as I decided to head back to my table on the patio.

I left the money on the bar as he set the glasses down in front of me. I balanced the three shot glasses in one hand and picked up my margarita in the other, taking a few sips as I walked toward the exit.

I should have been paying more attention because a burly guy suddenly stumbled into me with enough force to send me flying forward. In Shay's too-high heels, I could not catch my footing and was sure I would soon face-plant and end up with a margarita on my head and shot glass shards embedded in my hands.

Instead, a hand caught me and I collided with the firm chest of a man that smelled of mint and vanilla. Unfortunately, the contents of my drinks also collided with him.

Maybe it was the liquor, but instead of profusely apologizing, I started to giggle.

"So you think this is funny?" he said.

"No, I'm so sorry," I replied but couldn't keep my laughter in check. Red slush from my frozen margarita drizzled from the bottom of his shirt to the floor, and the shots left a large stain by the crotch of his shorts. "I'll pay for your dry cleaning," I offered, finally looking him in the eyes and becoming mesmerized by the perfection that was not just his smile, but his entire face.

"Don't worry about it," he said. "You're lucky my hotel's right across the street."

"And if it weren't?"

"If it weren't, I'd hold you hostage and command you to walk in front of me for the rest of the night."

"Well, at least I can hold my bladder for more than an hour," I said, giggling.

He asked me which line of adult diapers I'd recommend, since I was no spring chicken either. I liked that he shared my sarcasm. Not many people, aside from Shay, got my humor.

I often felt like the milk man's baby because my family was so serious. I would come up with the funniest one-liners, and they'd just stare blankly at me as if I was crazy. I felt like I was performing for a morgue. Even worse, my son's father would ridicule me when I tried to be funny, or he would take a joke too seriously and fly off the handle. I honestly stopped being myself in the years I spent with him, becoming very insecure and losing sight of myself.

Yet here was Lloyd, taking and throwing punches right alongside me. It turned me on even more than his good looks.

We kept talking, exchanging the basic name, age, where are

you from type of information. We found out we were both from New Jersey. Of course, he made fun of me for only having lived there for three years. He asked if I had ever "cruised" my stroller down the shore. I loved his Northern temperament.

Our witty banter was cut short when Shay came in, wondering where I'd disappeared to, and more importantly where the shots were that I was supposed to have procured. I explained to her that Lloyd saved me from the humiliation and injury of face-planting into the ground at the expense of his outfit and her shots.

"Well in that case, we owe *you* a drink. Do you and your friends want to join us at our table outside?"

"You bet. Let me grab them, and we'll meet you outside."

While Lloyd went to converse with his friends, I went with Shay to the bar. She ordered a pitcher of margarita and asked for extra cups. We took everything to our table on the patio.

Soon, Lloyd joined us with his more animated friend, Jax. The other guys stayed inside as they'd been picked to judge a wet t-shirt contest closer to the bar.

Jax took to Shay like clockwork, and the two of them flirted, barely paying any attention to the rest of us at the table. Melissa helped me get to know Lloyd a bit better, and of course took every opportunity to praise me as any good wingman would.

Before we knew it, the bartender was shouting for last call, and we were settling our bill.

"Well, it was great meeting you, Leann. I should go get changed and meet up with the rest of the guys. Could I get your number?"

I was reluctant to give it to him. He was mesmerizing, and we had a great time talking, but at the end of the day, I was still a mother. I needed to be there for my son. I had decided to be carefree and live it up for this trip, but in a few short days, I'd be back to real life and real responsibilities. Besides, Lloyd was four years older than me and was starting a promising career as a talent scout in New York, over *one-thousand miles* away. This could not go anywhere. Maybe it was best to cut my losses now.

"If we're meant to be, you'll find me again," I said as I walked away with Shay and Melissa.

"Nice line," Shay said when we were out of earshot. "Make him work for it. I'm sure we'll run into them again before we leave," she said with a sly smile.

That night, I tossed and turned in bed, thinking about Lloyd. Even though I knew we could not have a future together, I started to regret my decision not to give him my number. I increasingly hoped that somehow I would bump into him again before this trip was over. After all, I deserved a little fun.

The next night, we went to an outside beach-bar called Moe's. It took several pep talks and a shot of tequila to get me into a bikini and skimpy cover-up, but Shay insisted that Moe's was the place to be. Once we arrived, I was glad that I had sucked it up. It was so beautiful out. The stars glistened, and the moonlight pierced through the laminated palm trees that surrounded the deck of the bar. White string lights were wrapped around the deck, and the bar sat in front of a gigantic built-in fish tank highlighted with neon lights. My friends hit the dance floor with some locals they had met while I waited for a drink.

I looked around to scope out the scene and, to my astonishment, there he was, dressed in white pants and a white button-up shirt with the top buttons undone. I looked away quickly so that he would not catch me gawking at his perfect physique. My eyes met Shay's on the dance floor, and she mouthed a "you're welcome."

Jax must have told her where they would be tonight, and she set this up. I did not know whether to hug her or kill her in that instant.

So I threw back a shot of tequila and made my way to one of the empty beach chairs, not to Lloyd. It was not out of character for me to test fate over and over again.

As I looked up at the stars, I thought about my son. He was gorgeous in an obvious way. He had dark skin, maybe a shade darker than my olive complexion, black curly hair, and huge brown eyes. He had dimples that fit like quotation marks around his mouth. I wondered what he was up to and could hear his laugh in the distance. Then I thanked God that I had a boy as I noticed two teen girls dry humping each other one cabana over.

I sighed deeply, looking back up at the sky. Then, he appeared - Pedro, the Hispanic cabana boy.

"Shot, senorita?"

"Gracias." When free liquor was offered by a staff member, you didn't ask any questions. Just smile, and nod.

I took the shot then went to find my girls. I scanned the crowd and saw Melissa and Shay dancing in the center of the dance floor. Their moves were reminiscent of that scene from *Pulp Fiction*. I thought about rescuing them from embarrassment, but they were having a great time, so I decided to pretend I didn't know them instead. Although I did not want to harp on it, I noticed that I did not see Lloyd anywhere.

Had he left? Did I miss my shot? I was extremely disappointed and mad at myself for not going up to Lloyd when I saw him. *Why didn't I just kiss him when I had the chance? Why did I always have to test fate?* Now I would never get the chance again.

At that moment, two warm arms wrapped around me from behind. I instantly closed my eyes and smiled. Goosebumps grazed my arms, and I felt butterflies fluttering around in the pit of my stomach as I inhaled his minty-vanilla aroma.

Lloyd spun me around and greeted me with that big friendly smile. Before he could say a word, I kissed him. Everything around us faded out, the music stopped, the crowd silenced. At least, it did in *my* head. It was the most magical kiss I had ever experienced in my life.

♟♟

As memories of that first kiss with Lloyd still lingered on my mind, I realized I was still lying on a dirty New York street. I sprang up, hoping I hadn't gotten gum or something worse stuck on me. I checked my purse – wallet, keys, phone. Yup, good to go, and I finally hailed a cab.

As the cab approached my apartment, I took out my credit card and slid over behind the seat with the card reader to pay. I almost choked on the gum I had been chewing when I caught the driver's name on the ID tag that was taped to the windshield, "Lloyd." Get the fuck out of here. I believed in chance, even coincidence, but *come on*. Who names their Tajikistani son Lloyd?! It seemed like fate was trying to tell me something once again.

I paid my fare and went up to my apartment. My son arrived shortly after I got home. He was on winter break and spent the day with a boy from his class whose mother worked from home as a sales representative. I was friends with the other mothers in the building who also had boys around the same age as Lorenzo, and we would all help each other out a lot with the kids. Single motherhood seemed to be an epidemic for our generation. Only *two* of the seven mothers in the group had husbands. It was such a shame.

Occasionally on Saturday nights, I would watch the boys whose parents worked weekends or just needed a break. I loved cooking, and I was a true party planner at heart, something I inherited from my mother. I would always rent movies and make a bunch of pre-pubescent, boy-friendly foods. James, Pete, and

Jesse would be over this Saturday, and I made a note to pick up more peanut butter, pretzels, and pizza for them.

When Lorenzo entered the apartment, I greeted him as usual, bum-rushing him and tickling him. As a single mother to a boy, things could get rough. I could not count the times we played knee football (football on your knees) or slept in tents on the living room floor. Lorenzo, who I often called Renz, was starting to get older. He was not as welcoming to my affectionate gestures. Yet, despite his dire need to be "cool," I knew he still loved me.

"What do you want for dinner?"

"I ate at Jesse's."

I gave him a questioning look. My son was a picky eater, and I almost got offended when other mothers could get it right. Preparing his meals gave me a sense of joy because I was able to take care of my child and make him happy. In everyday life, I felt that so many things were out of my control, but at least this was one thing I was in control of – my child's food. After he reassured me that he wasn't hungry, he grabbed some video games and rushed off to James' apartment.

I had gotten used to his social life. While he was off being a boy, I was staying busy with my work. I knew a time would come when my son would start to transition from boy to man. I just did not expect that my mother would not be around to witness it. I realized that his way of coping with her loss was to throw himself into his friendships. Sometimes I felt he was avoiding me because being around me reminded him of her.

Although he adored me, I knew he loved my mother just as much. I could not blame him for that, and I understood that he was still grieving. Hell, I was too. I remembered how Lloyd brought me back to life in the days when I no longer felt alive. I was lost back then, and here I found myself lost again. I wished somehow, someway he could revive me again. I decided then and there to text him.

I was an avid number changer. Three to four times a year was no exaggeration in terms of my number-changing habits. Lloyd, on the other hand, had never changed his number in all the years that I knew him. I had no doubt in my mind that it would be the same. I entered the first four digits of his number, but then I erased them. I did this several times before I made it to the message itself, which consisted solely of a meek, "Hi. It's Leann."

Hi? Was that seriously what took me two hours to concoct? Before letting my insecurities kick in, I hit send and closed my eyes.

12

I buried my phone under a bunch of pillows because surely sending text messages meant opening up a gateway of transparency via our cell phones. I was still in last night's makeup and didn't want him to see me in this condition. I walked past the barricaded phone several times before checking it. When I finally looked, there was no reply yet. Hours passed and still nothing. Reality sunk in, he was over us.

I scrolled over to the texts that were saved under "Mom." I had all the "I love you" texts saved, along with many others. I told my mother anything and everything. I used to love springing the element of surprise on her. She was my best friend, and no one in the world knew everything about me but her.

I was thankful that my son was staying at James' tonight. James was Renz's best friend, and he lived in the apartment below us. I didn't want my son to see me bawling my eyes out. I always fought so hard to stay strong for him.

The next morning, Renz woke me with a hug. I guess the sprawled out tissues were a dead giveaway that I had a rough night.

"Ma, I need to get a book for a report at school."

Apparently, this book report should have already been in progress *before* winter break. But I was not opposed to using any excuse to buy a book for myself, so I decided to save the lecture about procrastination for another time. I loved reading and had even considered a career in writing. My mother and I had that in common. She wrote a couple of books, but had never gotten them published. Writing was something that I was definitely considering picking up again. It was therapeutic for me, and I could definitely use that now.

When we got to the bookstore, I was in heaven. I ran my fingers across the hard covers of the books as I walked. Keeping an eye on my overly energized boy and his friend Will, I walked over to the new releases section. One title in particular stood out, *Pawns of Love*. I did a couple of laps before returning to the face of that book. I picked it up and ran my fingers across the author's name. "L.L. Grellin." I was not familiar with her, but the title intrigued me - nothing like a good love story when you're having an early midlife crisis and overbearing emotions.

I thumbed to page one to gauge the writing style but did not get past the first sentence. Someone in a gorilla mask jumped in front of me, making monkey noises and waving their hands in my face.

"Ahh," I yelped, startled by the sudden intrusion in my space. Of course, it was Renz. He had again successfully scared the shit out of me. He loved catching me off guard. Like mother like son, I guess.

I grabbed the books that he and his friend had selected and decided to take the book I was holding as well. We got in line, and Renz started picking out odd, useless knick-knacks that the store bombarded you with at the checkout counter. I had a hard time saying no to Renz, so I allowed him to get a few pencils and erasers. I put my foot down though on the squeaky dog toy since we didn't have a dog and I didn't want Renz to get any ideas about asking me for one.

That night, the boys came over as planned and huddled in Renz's room playing video games. The boys took the occasional break to come out for snacks and to use the bathroom, but they pretty much kept to themselves at a decent noise level.

Meanwhile, I spent my Saturday evening mopping floors. In between the sways of the mop, I turned my phone off and on to make sure it was working properly. Then, I took to Facebook to see if I could find Lloyd. Again, there was nothing – not even a profile page. I knew he was not a big fan of social media, however, my paranoia made me wonder if he had blocked me from his account. We had not spoken in three long years. It was a messy break-up. Maybe that's why he was being so unresponsive.

What took me by surprise was that I did not hear from Lloyd when my mother passed. I wasn't sure that he even knew. My cell number had changed quite a few times in that three-year span, but my landline and address had remained the same until the New York move a few months ago.

As my eyes bounced over to the kitchen counter, I re-read the title of the book I had purchased. When I was with Lloyd, I used to love reading love stories. I tried to break him of his anti-fairytale syndrome. He would always say, "It's just a book. If people could write their own happy endings, then nothing would ever end – there'd be no divorce, no conflict, no death, and, more importantly, no make-ups or second loves. Perfection is boring." Maybe he had a point.

But I refused to let go of the fairytales. It wasn't until I found Lloyd that I fully worshipped something as seemingly unrealistic as the notion of soul mates. It was amazing how you could feel love from a person, even when they were absent. I knew not even death could break a bond like ours. Our relationship solidified my belief that there must be something after life ends. There was no way a feeling like this could be disposed of after life was over.

Besides, who was to say that the theory of soul mates could not be real when our whole belief system was based on the unimaginable? We were brought up being told about monsters, fairytales and Santa Claus. Then, at some point, the rug is pulled out from under us and we're taught that monsters don't exist, that fairytales are just make believe, and that whimsical characters such as Santa are really just our parents trying to bribe us into behaving. But do people forget that we are living on a huge ball that is spinning at a thousand miles per hour? Yeah, because a huge spinning orb called *Earth* is not odd at all.

I would not be deterred from my belief, not even by Lloyd, that love defies anything in the scope of understanding. It goes beyond anything that we are capable of comprehending, or even conjuring up. It is unimaginable. Therefore, fairytales could come true.

♟♙

Today had taken a toll on me. I was starting to argue politics and religious beliefs with myself. That's when I knew it was time to put the powdered donuts down and grab my book. After all, I had just convinced myself that fairytales *did* exist. Book in hand, I started toward my recliner. Then, the phone rang. It was Cheryl, James' mother. I anticipated this conversation putting me to sleep. Sundays were her days to entertain the boys, and she always called to "ok" her plans with me first.

Cheryl Deitz was a prissy, stuck up, Rhode Island native. As a widow, her parenting style was a little different from mine. Her motto was: "If it's not broken, it could get broken so we have to prevent it from being broken in the first place." Think of a sad little boy trapped in a bubble that his mother placed him in from birth. I somewhat understood that her husband's death had probably hit her hard, but it was seven years later. If it were up to her, she'd probably still be breastfeeding. My style of parenting was more casual. I felt you had to let a boy just be a boy.

She began, "Is it ok if Renz..."

I retorted, "Yes, yes, that's fine." I'm sure ice cream with gluten won't kill him. I wouldn't mention the Chinese food that most likely was made of cat that we ate the other night when James was over. Finally, I got her off the phone – ahh, finally, a moment of peace. I had endured way too many emotions in the

15

last forty-eight hours.

Aside from writing, reading had always been a great form of stress relief for me. As I nuzzled under a blanket on the couch, I braced myself for a good read. I opened the book up and began "Chapter One: They Meet." But before I could get more than two words in, the phone began ringing again. Cheryl must want to know if non-organic soda would be an issue, I thought.

To my dismay, it was someone I despised talking to more than Cheryl – my son's father. I had almost forgotten that Renz would be venturing to Florida for the summer to spend some time with his dad. Marc, Renz's father, was calling to discuss how we'd be splitting the cost of the plane ticket. Even though I had four months to prepare, the anxiety nearly overwhelmed me. I had no doubt in my mind that Renz would have fun and would be safe, but the thought of being without him was crippling. Although I wasn't a fan of Marc, I knew a boy needed his father. And Marc cleaned up his act a few years ago and eventually proved to be a standup father. He even apologized to me for the hell he put me through while we were together.

But seeing his name on my caller ID always took my mind to bad places before I could remember the good about him. At this moment, my thoughts went back to my first trimester with Renz. Marc was ripping me to shreds with his words, yelling that he could not sign over the rights to his unborn child fast enough. The outburst derived from a phone call that I overheard him having with his ex. He had come into his bedroom, the smell of rum rolling out of his mouth. I was laid across the bed preparing for what I thought would lead to a miscarriage. Marc and I had conceived previously, and the outcome was devastating. I thought for sure history would repeat itself.

As I lay nursing my cramps, he started rummaging through my purse, looking for my car keys. I felt disheartened because I knew what was to come. In a drunken stupor, he told me he was taking my car. At the time, his license was suspended, and he had no vehicle. I was, to say the least, infuriated. I knew exactly where he was going. What caught me off guard was that in my outpour of tears, there was no remorse in his eyes. He talked down to me like a dog.

But Marc wasn't always that way. He was a man–whore, yes, but the cruelty was something that he had managed to hide for the first year that I knew him. Maybe it had to do with the fact that I was unattached. It was in my second pregnancy with Marc that

I realized what a big mistake he was. I regretted getting involved with him, but I knew the reason fate had put him in my path, and that was to give me my son.

For years, I hated Marc for the verbal abuse he had showered me with. But at this point in my life, I could put my feelings aside and let him just be a father to his son, for which I was grateful.

I answered the phone cordially and worked out some of the remaining details regarding Renz's summer trip. Marc had given up drinking and cocaine, an addiction I wasn't even aware he had during most of our relationship. His attitude and behavior were no longer something I feared. He really was a decent guy when not weighed down by drugs and alcohol. He had been clean and sober for six years, and one of his first sober acts was to start building a relationship with Renz.

Sometimes, it took bad to appreciate the good. It took being broken by love, to accept being built up by it. It was the very loss of my own self that had led me to fall so hard for a person that had it all together. Lloyd was extremely smart. He had a business mentality about him that drew people in. He was articulate and determined. The go-getter attitude that he exerted was so sexy. He had a passion for life, and his drive rubbed off on me. His line of work revolved around productions. He was a talent agent who worked out of a small company in Manhattan. Most women would be insecure about their man being around models and "music video hoes" all day long, but Lloyd never made me feel that way. Something about the way he looked at me told me that no one else could compare.

CHAPTER TWO

Reminiscing

As I hung up the phone with Marc, I could not help but think of Lloyd. Both men had such an impact on my life that it was hard to think of one without my thoughts drifting to the other.

I remembered the first trip I took to New York. It was the first time I had seen Lloyd since Daytona. Our chemistry was undeniable, but believe it or not, we had not yet consummated our flirtations. The four nights we were in Daytona consisted of all-night conversations, comparing philosophies on life, and maybe a little foreplay here and there. We would watch the sun come up night after night, and I couldn't tell him then but I was already head-over-heels in love.

For four months, we kept in touch. We talked every day for hours about anything that came to mind. I felt as though Lloyd knew me better than some of my lifelong friends. There was no censor on how much of myself I was willing to show.

Lloyd was able to see into me; he saw the *real* me. It wasn't just his intelligence that captivated me – it was his ability to get a message across to someone as stubborn as myself. He taught me things and built me up in ways I didn't think were possible. He gave me a confidence that I had previously dropped and squished somewhere down the road.

For so long, I felt unseen and unheard, but with Lloyd I could finally reveal myself without anticipating rejection. He gave me the inner strength that I had always yearned for, and I thanked God for it.

When I stepped into his studio apartment in the East Village for the first time, things quickly escalated. I was worried that the time apart would have cultivated some awkwardness between us once we were finally in each other's presence again, but that fear quickly dissipated when his lips met mine.

Of course Lloyd was the perfect gentleman. He broke the kiss, took my coat and asked where I'd like to go for dinner. The fact that there was no pressure from him made me throw caution to the wind.

"I think we should order in," I said, then removed my top.

He stared at my chest for a few seconds with a look of adoration before closing the gap between us.

"I wish you could see yourself through my eyes," he said before pressing his lips to mine.

His hands roamed from my waist up my back. He paused as his fingers slid over the clasp of my bra, waiting for me to give the go-ahead. I did, and he let the strapless red garment fall to the floor. His hands fondled my breasts, first tenderly, then pinching my nipples lightly until I gasped.

There's a certain healing that comes from love. It's easy to fall for a person, but to relate to someone's soul is a sentiment reserved for *true* love. That night we made love for the first time, and although we had only known each other for a few months – most of which were spent apart – the connection we shared was undeniable and overwhelming.

We collided onto his bed, each of us in varied stages of undressed. The rest of our clothes were tossed in different directions around the room. A light sheen of sweat glistened over my body as his fingers inched up my thigh and finally found their way inside of me. I moaned in pleasure while his fingers brought me to the edge with expertise.

Passion for him coursed through my body, making me bold. I wrapped my legs around his waist and with a quick shift found myself on top. As I lowered myself onto him for the first time, his eyes scoured my body with a mix of pleasure and admiration. It was a look I would get to see many more times that night.

♟♟

A loud thud from my son's room broke me from my thoughts.

"What's going on in there?" I said as I hurried to Renz's room.

Luckily, no one was hurt, but a bookcase shelf and all of its contents had not survived a wild pass of a foam football from the other side of the room.

I warned them to stick to Madden on the Playstation only and put on my stern "Mom voice" to lay out the consequences if I found out about any more attempts at live action replays.

I returned to the living room, planning to finally start that new book, but all the thoughts racing through my head prevented me from being able to concentrate on the page. I sat the book in my lap as memories of Lloyd again filled my mind.

My escapades with Lloyd, early in our relationship, were usually limited to just one long weekend every month or two when one of us could make the trip to see the other. Lloyd always accepted my responsibilities as a mother, no questions asked. He understood that my son came first. Motherhood was undoubtedly my top priority, so I could not just traipse up and down the east coast whenever I pleased. Even though we could not visit each other often, we talked constantly on the phone, via text or over Skype.

Although our connection never wavered, the time and distance apart did take its toll. We could not be a traditional couple. I had to be a mom in Florida, and he had to get his career off the ground in New York. The result was a tumultuous on-again, off-again relationship status.

There was no question that we wanted to be together, but sometimes my insecurities or his jealousy would lead to arguments which led to shouting matches over the phone and hasty decisions to go on a break. But the pull between us was so strong that those breaks never lasted for more than a month or two.

Without fail, one of us would always make some extreme romantic gesture to win the other back. If he was at fault for the last argument, it would not be long before he showed up at my doorstep unannounced with tickets for a hot air balloon ride, backstage passes to the circus that was in town or some other creative outing that we could include Renz in. If I caused the last spat, I'd be at his place with something a lot more private and involving far fewer clothes planned for him. In all honesty, a phone call would have sufficed to put us back on track, but the passion and dramatics of it all helped get us through those long stretches we knew would come where we would not be able to see each other.

I glanced down and eyed the queen chess piece tattoo on my wrist. It was small and tasteful, nothing gaudy. Lloyd had the matching king piece on his wrist. I thought back to eight years ago when I got this ink.

♟♟

I hailed a cab outside of JFK airport and told the driver to take me to the Regis Grand Hotel. I sat in the backseat, biting my nails the entire drive. I was nervous. Lloyd had no idea I was in town, we had not spoken in five weeks, and it was December 30 so the city was on the brink of chaos with all the extra tourists in town to see the ball drop in Times Square.

The trip was impromptu and impulsive. My mom had won a New Year's in Times Square vacation package through a sweepstakes she entered at the mall and insisted that I use it to see Lloyd.

"I wouldn't be caught dead in that city this time of year with all those tourists," she said. "Besides, I can't take another day of looking at you moping around and pining for that boy. Go see him," she said, shoving a plane ticket into my hand.

"But—"

"But nothing. Go. Me and Renz have plans that don't include you anyway for New Year's," she said, winking at my son while actively pushing me out her front door. She handed me a folder. "There's a business card in there for the travel agent that set the giveaway up. Just call them and they'll let you know about the flight itinerary and hotel you'll be staying at. You leave in the morning so you need to hurry and get packed."

And with that, I was off to New York. Even though we had not spoken in weeks, I knew exactly where Lloyd would be for New Year's. My plan to surprise him, however, hinged heavily on Gwendolyn Rosario.

Gwen worked at the front desk of the St. James Hotel, which sat on the left shoulder of Times Square. Lloyd's production company often put prospective talent up in that hotel and held almost all of their company functions in the ballrooms and conference rooms there. So I had come across her often in the two years Lloyd and I had been seeing each other.

Gwen had naturally blonde hair that she peppered with black streaks. Her eyes were brown. She was short at 5'2" but athletically built. We would often crack jokes and exchange witty repartee while I waited for Lloyd to get a client settled or to get us a cab on rainy nights after work functions. But beyond random banter, we had never really had a full blown conversation.

Once I got checked into my room at the Grand Regis, I called the St. James and asked for Gwen. She was obviously surprised to hear from me, but luckily she at least remembered who I was.

"I know it may be asking too much, but you've helped Lloyd and his coworkers out with last-minute requests before, and I was hoping to ask a favor of you to help me surprise Lloyd. He doesn't know I'm here."

"Um, ok. What kind of favor?" she asked hesitantly.

I proceeded to lay out my plan to her. Once I finished, I held my breath, hoping she wouldn't hang up on me. After a few seconds of silence, I started to think she had hung up.

"Hello… Gwen, are you still there?"

"That is so romantic. Of course, I'll help," she squealed.

I let out a sigh of relief and listened as she perfected my game plan and told me when and where to meet her.

♟♟

It was 11:45, minutes before the New Year would ring in, and I was freezing my ass off on the open-air observation deck on the 86th floor of the Empire State Building. I know, very *Sleepless in Seattle*, but I was without a doubt sleepless in Florida so it seemed appropriate and romantic. But as it was getting closer to midnight, I was starting to worry that Gwen may have overestimated her powers of persuasion to get Lloyd up here.

11:50… 11:55… Damn it. *What was I thinking?* Of course Lloyd couldn't leave his office New Year's Eve party. He would for sure be schmoozing new clients. Plus, why would he want to leave? It was one of the hottest parties going on in the city tonight. Even if he wanted to leave, the crowds would make it near impossible to commute anywhere. Why didn't I just tell him I was in town? I could be warm and in his arms right now at that party.

"I'm such an idiot," I said out loud.

"I'd have to disagree," a voice said from behind me.

I whipped around to see Lloyd holding a bottle of champagne and two glasses, each with a strawberry in them.

"So I'm guessing Gwen's story about an A-list client demanding a champagne delivery wasn't quite on the up and up," he said, popping the bottle and filling the two glasses. "And if it was, well, they're not getting it now," he said with a smirk.

People around us started cheering, and I saw the ball begin

its descent. "10, 9, 8," the crowd screamed. I had to get closer to Lloyd so he could hear me.

"I hope you're not disappointed to just find little old me here," I replied.

He handed me a glass of champagne and put the bottle down near his feet.

"3, 2, 1!"

Fireworks lit up the sky and the screams and cheers were deafening, but the only sense I could register was touch as Lloyd kissed me.

"Happy New Year," he finally said when our lips parted.

"I love you," I blurted out, not thinking. It was the first time I had uttered those three little words to him.

Realizing what I'd done, I quickly downed my glass of champagne, part of me hoping he had not heard me. Although we'd known each other for two years, we had probably spent less than two months' worth of time actually in each other's presence – couple that with our breaks and the fact that he was a man – and I was worried that my words would scare him off. We hadn't spoken for five weeks after all.

Before my mind could run rampant with more worries, Lloyd lifted my chin so he could look me in the eyes. "I've always loved you," he said.

I could not help the biggest grin from spreading across my face. We finished the champagne then made our way to the St. James. Before we got there, we saw an open tattoo parlor.

"What do you think?" Lloyd suggested. "Should we commemorate this night forever?"

Instead of answering, I kissed him, and then pulled him into the parlor.

"What should we get?" I asked him while taking in all the artwork on the walls and beginning to peruse a catalog of the artist's past work.

"Well, I heard this quote recently. 'Every man needs a woman when his life is a mess because, just like in a game of chess, the queen protects the king.' I'm not sure who said it, but it resonated with me. I think we should get king and queen chess pieces."

"But you know the queen's not protecting the king; she's keeping the opposing queen from flirting with her man," I joked, loving that he was back to his chess metaphors.

"Ha ha. Very funny. Seriously though, the queen is the most powerful piece on the chessboard, but it has nothing to do with her ability to move all over the board. It's the sacrifices she is willing to make to save her king's life that makes her so commanding," Lloyd said. "That mix of strength, beauty and intelligence exemplifies you, babe."

"I love it, and I love you. King and queen chess pieces it is," I said.

We took seats in the waiting room to plan out the exact design. An hour later, we were at the St. James and the party there was still roaring on. Before we hit the dance floor, I went to find Gwen. She was still at the front desk, and I thanked her profusely for helping me pull this night off. From that point on, our mere acquaintance began to morph into a lifelong friendship. Her shift was almost up and Lloyd insisted that she join the party as his guest as soon as she was able to clock out. The three of us partied like rock stars until dawn.

♟♟

It was truly an unforgettable night. Considering the way things panned out for Lloyd and I, some might think that I would regret the tattoo. In actuality, I cherished it. It was a reminder of a night and a time in which I was truly happy.

A police siren outside snapped me out of my past and back to the present. I went to check on the boys, and they were passed out. I turned off their television and got them tucked in, then headed to my bedroom.

After a quick shower, I crawled under the sheets but could not fall asleep. Between thoughts of Lloyd, my son's trip and my mom, my mind would not shut down.

Renz's upcoming trip would be his first time back to Florida since his grandmother died. I had asked Renz if he was going to visit her grave. He said he could not face that without me. I knew that I should have been planning to accompany him to ease his grieving, but my own grief was standing in the way. The guilt ate away at me, but I just wasn't ready.

Images from my childhood started racing through my mind. Block parties in New Jersey, watching my mother and father sing Beatles songs with their friends while simulating guitars with mops and brooms. I pictured my mother and me baking Christmas cookies in our first Florida home. I saw my mother hanging Christmas lights outside of our house, ladder and all. People would often come from miles to see the light show, nativity scene, and other décor my mother produced. It really was beautiful. We should have made the news or at least had a spot in the paper.

My mother was like wonder woman. She did everything that was expected of a woman and then turned around and handled the tasks of a man. Not that my father didn't handle his business. He was the breadwinner while my mother stayed home when we were kids. My father busted his ass working two jobs to give my mother the luxury of being a stay at home mom. I think my father's absence in my childhood due to his hectic work schedule affected me more than I'd ever like to admit. I know he loved us, but he was not one to let his emotions show often. Hugs and I love you's were the sole domain of my mother.

My mother was a bit of a pushover. She was a shy woman that always went the extra mile for her family. My father, brother, and I were all very dependent on her. Although she would often complain about her heavy workload, I think she loved being so needed. My mother kept up her duties as a wife and a parent, went through nursing school once my brother and I were older, and then became a successful career woman. She was capable of anything and never needed help from anyone. I envied that about her.

Depending on my mother so much, in a way, caused me to lack independence in adulthood. I mean, I didn't know how to write a check until I was... I'll get back to you on that. Or, I'm still forgetful when it comes to making my own dentist appointments.

This lack of dependence gave me even more of a reason to admire Lloyd. He was forced to be dependent at a very young age, taking on chores like the laundry at age seven. It was something I couldn't grasp. My mother had still been getting me drinks and catering to me throughout my *twenties.*

Lloyd's upbringing had not been as charmed as mine. His father had walked out on him and his mom when he was four years old. Our first argument as a couple actually stemmed from some unresolved feelings he had about his father while I was going on a tirade about my dad not being emotionally available.

Renz had finger-painted him a picture for his birthday. When my son handed him the picture, he looked at it for a second, said "That's nice," put it on the refrigerator, and walked away. I could tell Renz was disappointed that his gesture didn't garner more of an outwardly loving reaction from his grandfather. My mother also noticed and swooped Renz up in her arms and asked him lots of questions about his painting, who was in it, and why he picked the colors, all the while showering him with praise.

"Can you believe that?" I told Lloyd over the phone that night. "I mean, what kind of man does that to a three-year-old?"

"Just because he doesn't show affection how you want him to show it, doesn't mean he doesn't care or isn't a good man. He put it on the refrigerator. That showed Renz that he appreciated the drawing and was proud of it," he responded.

"Please. A three-year-old needs more than that. I can't believe you're taking his side," I yelled.

"I'm not taking sides, Leann. Damn, you're being a spoiled brat," he said, slighting raising his voice.

"How dare you call me a brat! I -"

He cut me off. "You should be thankful you have a father that not only stuck around to raise and care for you, but is now doing the same for your son."

I shut up immediately. I couldn't believe how insensitive my gripe, over something that was admittedly probably an overreaction on my part, with my father was to someone who had really been wronged by their father. I would never understand what it felt like to have the man who was supposed to love and protect me forever choose to leave without a word. Although my father and I did not have the most open relationship, I knew that he'd be there for me with open arms if I needed him.

Lloyd deserved full credit for pushing me into womanhood. He challenged me to do better, to do more. And I was eager to impress him, so pushing myself harder was the only option. He didn't know it at the time, but he always kept me striving for more.

Lloyd was four years my senior and exactly what I would expect out of a grown man. I was always concerned with how his view of me was shaping up. I guess it's something I had picked up early on in life – constantly worrying about being good enough. It wasn't long after we met that Lloyd caught on to my spoiled nature. "Brat" was a term of endearment that I'd never live down.

While reminiscing about my mother, I began to think of others that I had lost. Loss was not unfamiliar ground for me. I had endured several losses over the course of my life. I started to focus on my mother's father. He was the first person I had ever lost. I remembered being too afraid to deal with saying goodbye, so I didn't. Typical Leann, ignore and sweep it under the rug. Maybe then it would go away. Maybe then it wouldn't be so *real*.

I think my coping mechanisms are what eventually led me to

become unafraid of death. My grandfather would always say that living was Hell, and dying was living. Those words have never left me. It only made sense that a world of pain would be hell – to finally rest would be a heaven, a calming thought to any mind.

I used to believe my heaven was in New Jersey on Cherry Street. Across from our home were my dad's parents, my aunts and uncles, and next door from them were my mom's parents, aunt, uncle, and cousins.

We would have countless block parties, get-togethers in the basements, and Italian-styled holiday dinners that lasted all night. As a child, I would pray for my family and I to live forever. If that wasn't possible, I at least wanted us to all go out together. End of the world? Freak accident? Whatever, I'd take it. As I got older, I still had all of my family members while my friends weren't as lucky. I did not know one person that had both sets of grandparents. I thought for sure that God and I had an understanding.

My belief that God and I had the best kept secret came to a halt when my mom's father died. It was days before my sixteenth birthday when he went. He was on hospice and he was in our home in Florida. I hid out in my room until it was all over and never stopped living with regret. It was the first dead body I had ever seen. The shock of it all took me back a little. I had learned to accept death as a fact of life by the time my mother's mother passed. I was twenty-two, and my grandma was following the fate of her late husband. She was in our home, on hospice, and I wouldn't make the same mistake twice. It was bittersweet to take care of my grandmother as she once had done for me.

She always was a hard-ass to a fault, tough and uncompromising. She felt as though crying was a weak trait. Near the end, she sat physically weak, yet mentally strong. I overheard her tell my mom that she was concerned with how I felt about having to care for her. Here she was, at the end of her life, and she was worried about *me*. I sat with her, painted her nails, wet her dry lips. It was a beautiful, sacred moment and I'm glad that I was there to hold her hand until the very end.

As my life went on, a new perception of heaven developed in my mind. Had my original theory on heaven been correct, then my son and Lloyd wouldn't have been accounted for. That childhood vision no longer held weight. Lloyd was undoubtedly my soul mate, but if such was true then there had to be such a thing as a soul child. I know, the R&B singer popped into my head too, but seriously, Renz was meant to be in my life then and in all the lives to follow.

My son had been put into my life for a reason. He was in many ways my saving grace. When my mother died, I couldn't tell who the child was and who the parent was. He was so strong for me, so grown up.

There was one night I didn't leave my bedroom, and as he'd check up on me I would pretend I was asleep. At one point in the night, I felt him kiss my cheek and cover me with my blanket. Renz took care of me just as much as I took care of him. Now he was to be taking his first trip without me.

♟♟

I thought about the first time Renz and Lloyd met. Renz was three years old at the time, and a little spitfire to say the least. He was hard to handle. Marc had been involved with his son but only at his convenience – only if he didn't feel like drinking. I wished so desperately that I would have made better choices. Not for myself, but for my son's sake. He deserved so much more than a part-time dad who was absent from both of our lives much too often.

A psychic I had seen when I was eighteen told me I would have one child, and the child's father would not be involved. Maybe my hoop earrings, too tight top and itty bitty skirt were a dead giveaway that I went for the wrong type of guy. Nonetheless, I was intrigued. I reported everything the psychic told me to my good friend Jayde. I told her that the psychic revealed I was involved with the wrong people and that if I didn't keep my distance from that crowd, I would end up dead because of it. I remembered the look on her face when I told her, and the response she gave me now gives me chills. Jayde told me she had this awful gut-feeling that the reading I received could also have been applied to her.

Jayde was a mother to a beautiful little girl approaching her first birthday. Jayde was absolutely gorgeous: she had beautiful brown eyes, long brown hair, and the perfect smile. She had a sense of humor like mine, but unlike me she had her shit together at such a young age. Her parents were struggling with their own demons so she succeeded in becoming an emancipated minor when she was sixteen. She was a great mother, a great woman.

As she revealed her belief that the reading was for her, she said something else to me that would go unnoticed at the time. She said she could not visualize her daughter or herself being any older. Months later, she was fatally shot when the convenience store she worked at was held up.

I remembered how long it took me to muster up the courage to let Lloyd meet Renz. I knew one day that Lloyd would be an incredible father, but I was hesitant to bring him into Renz's life. What if it didn't work out in the long run for Lloyd and me? What if Renz got attached, and then became disappointed, or worst of all, what if my son didn't like him?

Lloyd flew down to Florida for the meeting. We met him at the airport. He had a toy lion, zebra, and monkey in his hands. My son was going through a zoo animal stage. It became routine for him and I to crawl around the floor and growl at each other each night. My son would somehow throw pig noises into the mix. Little did Lloyd know, he'd soon be joining us.

We got closer to Lloyd and, to my astonishment, Renz took right to him. He usually shied away from new people, but he was crazy about Lloyd – just as crazy as I was about him.

I had been having a little trouble disciplining my son, and I inherited the "give 'em whatever they want" trait from my mother. On Lloyd's last night in town, we went to a Spanish bistro on the water. Before the second course, my son decided to throw his scheduled dinnertime fit. I turned red on the spot as my inability to control my child humiliated me. I pondered slipping under the table – maybe no one would even know I was gone.

I looked over at Lloyd and told him to pass my plate under the table when it arrived. As I half-jokingly lifted up the tablecloth, he took my hand and gave me that hypnotizing grin. He had this effortless way to put my mind at ease. In a gentle, yet stern dictation he told my son to behave or else he wouldn't get dessert. Now my son may have not known the word "no," but he definitely knew the word "dessert" very well. Renz complied, no eye rolling, no punching Lloyd in the gut as he did with me, and I was impressed. Lloyd didn't know it, but in this moment I fell even more in love with him for his quiet grace in dealing with difficult situations.

It was not until recently that I discovered my mother had the same admiration for Lloyd as I did. Through the years I had only let them get to know each other from a distance. She witnessed flower deliveries on my birthday, and she even received some each Mother's Day, thanking her for creating me. But because I had gone through so many tumultuous relationships, I just wanted to protect all parties from any further disappointments.

That's why I kept Lloyd hidden to an extent.

Throughout my life, my mother had kept journals for my brother and me to read when we were older. She wanted us to have a firsthand account of what she considered our best moments. When we had children of our own, she started journals for them too. In each journal, she would write us yearly letters. I had only recently mustered up enough strength to read mine. I was in awe of how proud I made her. The letters drove me to tears. They said things like, "I always knew she could do it, my little girl is a firecracker," and "Leann just drew the most miraculous picture today, she has such a talent." In her last letter before her passing, she wrote "marry that man." As I read that passage I felt a warm, calming presence surround me. I believe that she finally understood what I had known for years about Lloyd – he was the *one*.

♟

I flashed back to my first time taking Renz to New York. My son was an animated six-year-old. He would sing and dance, and he was pretty damn good at it. Now I'm not just saying this because he's my son; the boy had talent. I decided my son should be seen. He had the ability to captivate people, and I thought his talents were exceptional. And who better to help us out than Lloyd? Lloyd had arranged for us to meet with some of his agent friends in New York. I was so excited to show my son this completely different world. He had never been to a big city. I'd taken him to Tampa a few times, but that could not go to bat with NYC.

After some careful consideration, I decided to bring Shay along. Shay had never been to NYC either and I wanted her to finally meet Gwen, the lifesaver who made that New Year's Eve outing possible.

As the plane took off, Renz and Shay peered over me to see out of the window. I shut my eyes and tried to get some rest while the two of them made a commotion out of excitement.

I knew how amazing this experience would be for the two of them. When we landed, we quickly retrieved our bags, then jumped into a cab. I warned them of the NYC style of driving, but they were oblivious to anything coming out of my mouth, oohing and ahhing in sync with each other as they took in the sights. As we entered the city, both of their faces were stuck to the window like love bugs to a Florida driver's windshield.

The tall buildings engaged them, and they kept trying to push each other out of their peripherals. I laughed to myself at this very special moment. As we approached our hotel, the St. James, of course, Gwen ran out to hug me.

"Your son is so handsome," she said in her New York accent and knelt down to give him a high five.

My son, being the Casanova he was, developed an instant crush on her. I introduced Gwen to Shay, and Shay sort of sized her up. It was endearing how protective and territorial Shay was of me.

We all unloaded our stuff and met Lloyd at one of our favorite restaurants down the block. Lloyd was "in" with all the big wigs, and business was his business. When I was on-site with him, we got VIP everything. Sometimes it reminded me of how the Italian wise-guys would always snap and get whatever they wanted. We walked into Melbourne's Steak House and were ushered to private seating in the back. Lloyd was already at the bar with some local entertainers.

Renz ran over to Lloyd, and Lloyd gave him a big bear hug, which of course turned into some light playful sparring. Renz absolutely adored Lloyd. He looked up to him in a way he didn't even look up to his own dad. They shared a significant bond that I deeply appreciated. We all sat down and had a beautiful dinner. It was exciting for Shay and Renz, but even more so for me to be sharing this with them. Even though I lived in Florida, NYC always felt like home to me.

The next day we invaded all the cliché New York attractions. Lloyd was working, so he arranged for a limo to take us sightseeing. We saw the Empire State Building, and I smiled as I remembered the first time I told Lloyd I loved him there. We did lunch in Central Park. We even went to a couple museums. The best part of our sightseeing was coming across the FAO Schwarz toy store. I was with two children, so they absolutely loved it.

The next day Renz was to meet with a top New York agent. Lloyd insisted that he take him and I stay behind because this agent was known for having a warden-like temperament. I disagreed at first. I wanted to be there for my son, but Lloyd reiterated that only one adult could escort the talent and that he had "pull," as he called it. Although I was somewhat pissed off, I obliged.

Shay and I went off to get our palms read by one of the most prestigious psychics in all of Manhattan. Okay, it was very common for me to try to obtain the answers to life's unattainable questions. My free spirit had me in constant search for new-aged healings. I had dabbled in Chinese medicine such as acupuncture, I had gone organic for a week or two when I was twenty-three, and I had also spent a good month, okay summer, stalking a local psychic. Even though Lloyd didn't believe in any of my zany antics, he supported my need to find answers.

While in Atlantic City the summer before, Lloyd had even taken his support to the next level. He kept babbling about how lucky he felt, surely he'd win big. As we roamed the boardwalk just outside of the Taj Mahal, I told him there was only one way to find out. Pointing to a neon sign that read Madame Wassel, I ushered him inside. After a brief but elaborate reading, he wasn't cracking. She told him we would have seven children and three dogs. Lloyd was allergic to dogs. Then she told him he was an emperor in a previous life, which he believed.

As we paid the lady and made our way out of her embroidered handmade tent, Lloyd looked over at her and in a lispy voice said, "My man is gonna be so upset by these revelations." He snapped in an overly dramatic drag-like manner, and we were off. We spent the rest of our walk cracking up at the expression on the psychic's face.

After Shay and I returned from our outing, Renz and Lloyd returned with great news. The talent agent wanted Renz to be the new face of a children's clothing line. As appreciative as I was, I questioned what had happened at the agency. Neither of them ever told me. Renz's gig was short lived. Although he did some print work, and made enough money to for a sizeable college fund, it wasn't his passion. He was a boy and wanted to get dirty with his friends. I let him know if it was something he ever wanted to pursue down the road, to let me know. I made sure he knew I was his biggest cheerleader, and whatever he wanted to do was fine with me.

♟

I finally dozed off, thinking of Renz. Unfortunately, I was also woken up by him at far too early an hour for the weekend. I checked my phone and, to my dismay, Lloyd still had not responded. I could not dwell on that though. I had hungry boys to feed.

By noon, James, Pete, and Jesse had all gone home. Renz was in his room, working on his book report and some other school work. The house was too quiet, and I was restless. Some stress cleaning was in my future. As I got my cleaning supplies together in an assembly-like rotation, I decided to call Gwen.

"Spill it," Gwen said, cutting off my failed attempt at small talk. "I can tell something's weighing on you."

"Well, umm, I texted Lloyd," I said.

"What? What did he say?"

"That's the thing. He didn't text back."

"Say no more. I get off work at four, and then I'm coming straight over."

Until then, I busied myself burning sage and ridding the apartment of toxins. Renz emerged from his room a few times for snacks, but it was otherwise quiet. James stopped by just before four to ask if Renz could spend the night at his house. I called Cheryl, and she said she was happy to keep the boys and get them off to school in the morning. I packed Renz' overnight bag and sent him on his way.

Gwen was knocking on my door shortly after, wine in hand, ready to relax and detox with me. We sipped pink Moscato and started dusting the bookcases. Gwen was well aware of my stress cleaning habits, so she did not try to stop me. I knew she was itching to ask about Lloyd but was waiting for me to bring it up. I didn't really know what to say. I texted, and he didn't reply. We weren't together, so I had no right to expect anything from him. I didn't even know for sure whether that was still his number.

Rather than bring it up, I started straightening the magazines and knick-knacks on the coffee table. The book I'd picked up at the bookstore, *Pawns of Love*, was on the table, and I made a mental note to start reading it, as I went on cleaning. But soon the wine started to do its magic, and my lips loosened up.

"I... I can't believe he really didn't text back," I mumbled, starting to get teary-eyed. "Have you seen him lately, like with a client at the hotel?"

"Oh, sweetie, you can't let this bring you down. We've already done the mourning for that relationship, and there's no need to start that again. And, no, I haven't seen him. His company expanded their West Coast office, and I heard he moved out to Los Angeles. But the company's contract with the hotel ended last year, and they didn't renew so I haven't seen much of that crowd in a long time."

"You're right. I don't know why I'm letting all these feelings and wounds open back up."

"Renz is out and taken care of for the night, right? Let's get out of here. Why don't we hit up Tavern Blue? We haven't been there in ages," Gwen suggested.

Gwen did not know it, but that was one of the last places I wanted to be, especially if the goal was to not think about Lloyd.

Tavern Blue was a club that Gwen and I used to frequent a lot. However, I had not been there in almost four years. I paused. Acknowledging the last time I was there meant acknowledging what had brought me there. It was a memory I had buried. It was the beginning of the end for Lloyd and me, and I could no longer prevent the memories from flooding in. I threw back my wine and finally allowed myself to face the demise of my relationship with Lloyd.

CHAPTER THREE

Off-Season

The Tavern Blue had been the precursor to many steamy nights with Lloyd. Maybe it was the dark setting, high quality drinks or proximity to other bodies glistening with sweat, but after a night at that club, Lloyd and I usually couldn't get back to his place fast enough.

The particular night in question took place four years ago, our inhibitions were at an all-time low. We started kissing in a booth near the back. My hands had found their way under Lloyd's shirt, while his fingers kept creeping up my thigh until they rested just beneath the hem of my dress. It was dark, and we were mostly out of sight. Yet, we were cognizant enough of our surroundings to stop us from ripping each other's clothes off right there. Things, however, had gone too far to put on the brakes and trek back to his place.

Lloyd broke our kiss and motioned his head to the corner behind us. It was the men's room. I nodded and followed behind him. When no one seemed to be looking, we both slipped in and made a beeline for the largest stall we could find. I started to get nervous when I heard the man who had been at the urinal start to chuckle, but he just washed his hands and quickly left the restroom.

I didn't have much more time to think after that, as Lloyd dropped to his knees, lifted up my dress and proceeded to rip my panties off. I gasped, my mind was no longer concerned with our location or who might be able to hear us. Lloyd put his tongue to work and in minutes I was hitting my climax.

"I love the sounds you make, baby, almost as much as I love the taste of you," Lloyd said, licking me off of his lips.

His words made my knees quiver, but I regained my composure quickly. Knowing we could be interrupted at any moment, I wanted to make sure he got as much out of this escapade as I did.

I turned away from him and positioned my hands on the stall door for support. My dress was hiked well above my waist so he had a perfect view of my backside as I bent over slightly. I looked over my shoulder to see him taking in the view with admiration and lust. He had unzipped his pants and was sliding a condom on.

"You think you can handle this?" I said teasingly, wiggling my rump and giving him a wink.

I planned to continue the teasing and throw in some playful banter and dirty talk, but before I could get another word out, he plunged inside of me with one quick thrust.

I let out a loud moan as our bodies meshed perfectly. His firm hands grasped my waist and pulled me closer to him with each thrust. I was awash with pleasure and lost myself in his rhythm once again.

I wanted this – not just the sex but the closeness with him, the physical proximity – to never end. But it always did. One of us always had to catch a flight back home – because our homes were not one and the same. In fact, I would be on a flight back to Florida the next afternoon.

"I don't want this to end," I whispered to Lloyd.

"It's not going to," he said. "Let's just get back to my place first before we get thrown out, or worse, someone calls the cops on us," he said, laughing.

"That's not what I mean," I said, taking on a more serious tone, at least as serious as one could be with the amount of shots that were still coursing through my system. "We work, Lloyd. Not just in the bedroom, or er… the bathroom as may be the case. But what we have is worth more than constant phone calls and stolen moments together every few weeks. We need to be in the same city."

The look he gave me was one I'd seen countless times before. We'd had this conversation already, and I knew now was not the time to have it again, but I just couldn't help it. The alcohol mixed with our passion for each other was overwhelming, and I couldn't hold in what I was feeling, even if it was sure to kill the mood.

"We have to get out of here," Lloyd said, grabbing my hand and leading me out of the restroom.

He seemed to be leading me to the dance floor. I guess he was hoping I'd get hopped up on pheromones again and drop the conversation. That made me angry. I released his hand.

"We need to talk about this, Lloyd," I said, slightly raising my voice.

I thought about the fights that preceded this trip. They were constant. I had been pressing him to move to my city, and he had been telling me it wasn't possible but he'd love for Renz and me to move to New York with him.

But I did not want to uproot Renz from his friends and family. He was very close to my mother, and so was I. Leaving her was not an option. For years, the distance and time spent apart were things we ignored and insisted did not matter. We shared a naïve belief that love would conquer all, as cliché as that sounds.

But things were changing. Lloyd wanted to run his own production company. He had some leads to get things started in New York, but there were far better prospects shaping up for him in Los Angeles. When it had first come up, I tried to play the role of supportive girlfriend and didn't share my concerns. But the thought of even more distance between us had been gnawing at me for a while.

Besides, why ask me to move to New York with him if he was considering a cross-country move himself? Didn't he understand that I had a child to put first? I couldn't just bring Renz to New York one minute, then have to relocate again to LA the next. He had school and needed stability. And new companies, ones in the entertainment business at that, were always risky. What if his company didn't take off, and he needed to move again? I could not put Renz through that type of upheaval.

The sober me knew that Lloyd was very considerate of Renz's needs and that it wasn't smart or plausible for Lloyd to just drop his whole career for us, but the inebriated me didn't care and lacked a filter.

"If you really loved me and Renz, you'd stop making business your number one priority and put *us* first. You'd come back to Florida with me," I said.

"Baby, now is not the time—"

"Don't 'baby' me," I said, cutting him off. "And when will it be the time? I mean, it's been eight years! Why are we still telecommuting this relationship?" I yelled at him.

"I can't just drop my whole life," he said, loudly. He was clearly getting irritated with me. "I have to make a living. What sense would it make for me to come to a small town with no job prospects for me?"

"It makes sense to be near the ones you love," I countered. "Or is that too much for you? It's convenient to have this pseudo-family with me and Renz that you can check in and out of as you please, isn't it?"

My insecurities were bubbling over. A part of me always worried about Lloyd's commitment. Nagging thoughts about who he spent time with when I wasn't around, what female company he kept when we were on our breaks, and whether he would still be into me if he had to put up with me on a regular basis would occasionally overpower my resolve that Lloyd was the *one* for me. This was one of those times. And the alcohol made things worse.

"Like father, like son, I guess. Can't deal with a real commitment?" The moment I said it, I regretted it. But I was too drunk to immediately apologize and take it back.

"What the hell did you just say?" he shouted.

I had crossed a line. Lloyd worked hard and wanted to be able to provide for me and Renz, so I knew he had no intentions of settling down in a small Florida town. It was either I went to New York, or nothing at all. But I simply could not comply with that. I'm sure he thought I was being selfish, but what I was doing was far more *selfless* than he realized.

I could not put my own happiness above my son's. My poor choices had already saddled him with a less than stellar father. I could not drag him along for this ride with Lloyd while there were so many uncertainties. But what I said to Lloyd was uncalled for. I knew his father was a sore topic for him. Bringing him up and accusing Lloyd of being like him – a man that could walk out on his family, leaving them with nothing – took this argument to a full-blown shouting match in the middle of the club.

"How about you grow up, Leann? We both know the only reason you won't move to New York is because you're so damn scared of leaving your mother. Try taking care of yourself and your kid without leaning on your mother so much," he yelled at me.

Things continued to escalate until I ran out of the Tavern Blue crying. Lloyd was only a few feet behind, following after me. But I didn't want to talk anymore. A cab was out front, and I hopped in before Lloyd could catch up to me. I slipped the driver an extra $20 to get me to Lloyd's apartment as fast as he could. I wanted to get in and out, to retrieve my luggage, before Lloyd could make it home. The driver did as requested, and I was there in record time. He waited out front of Lloyd's building for me to grab my things, then took me to a hotel near the airport. I took the cheapest room they had available and immediately crashed into the hotel bed, crying myself to sleep.

I ignored Lloyd's texts and calls the next day and boarded my flight back home without speaking to him. I continued to ignore his attempts at communication for the next few weeks until the calls and texts stopped coming.

The distance had finally gotten to be too much, and there was no way to fix it. I could not uproot my son, and he could not risk his career. I reasoned that we would only keep hurting each other.

♟♙

Four months was the longest duration of time we had ever gone without speaking to one another before our big fight at Tavern Blue. Seven months had now lapsed. But in that time, my resolve regarding our split had weakened.

I had gotten so used to the on-and-off nature of our relationship that even close to a year's time didn't seem like an unattainable comeback. We had grown accustomed to delicate chess maneuvering in our relationship. We had both seen other people during our extended off-seasons in the past, but we both knew what moves to play to win back each other's heart. So I was confident that I'd feel the warmth and strength of Lloyd's arms around me soon when I made the decision to take a trip to New York and surprise him. I had no idea the game was about to be over though, for good.

Although I was confident that Lloyd would take me back, I was still nervous and indecisive about whether that was ultimately a good idea. The distance was still an issue. My apprehension exhibited itself through a cycle of packing, unpacking, and then repacking.

Shay offered to come along for moral support, and I was glad to have the company. We both had a few extra days off work due to the upcoming Fourth of July holiday so we settled on that long weekend to travel and found flight deals. I reached out to Gwen for a discounted room at the St. James.

On the flight to New York, I tried to visualize how the trip would go. A psychic once told me that visualization could be used as a tool to help shape the universe in your favor. I figured nothing could hurt at this point. I pictured arriving in New York and relaxing in the hotel hot tub with Shay. Once Gwen was off work, we'd hit up the hotel spa services so I would be sure to look my best for my reunion with Lloyd. I envisioned our eyes meeting, and Lloyd running up to me and picking me up as he often did out of excitement. It was going to be a beautiful, long-awaited embrace. I was getting excited the more I fell into this fantasy, which was taking a turn toward a toe curling, mountain moving romp in the sack.

I started to think that maybe there really was some power to visualization. The trip started just as I'd hoped. After our spa appointment, Gwen suggested we do some shopping to find me what she called an "Operation: Win Lloyd Back" dress. I didn't know why my friends always thought that my clothes weren't skimpy or sexy enough. Sure, I was a mom, but I thought my wardrobe was comparable to any twenty-seven-year old's. Nevertheless, I went along with the shopping excursion. I really just wanted an empanada and knew we'd pass this great Argentinean bakery while out and about.

After browsing through the third boutique and still not finding that perfect dress, I was starting to get discouraged. Maybe this was a sign that it wasn't the right time to re-enter Lloyd's life. I mean, who couldn't find a hot dress in New York? My spirits rose a bit as I held my head up and saw that the Argentinean bakery was on the next corner.

"It's time for a snack break, ladies," I announced. "Who's up for chicken empanadas?"

"Girl, you're the only one I know who can scarf down carbs like it's nothing, and go back to trying on tight dresses without a problem," Gwen said.

"What can I say? I have a high metabolism," I replied, laughing, as we walked toward the bakery.

The girls continued to chastise me about my eating habits as we got closer to the bakery.

"On my god," I said as we reached the corner, and I stopped dead in my tracks. The bakery was right across the street, but I could not believe what I was seeing.

"What? You know we're joking with you. You had a baby and

snapped back to a size four in all of two seconds," Shay said.

"No, it's not that. Look," I said, pointing to the window. There sat Lloyd.

"Well, there's no time like the present," Gwen said.

"But… but… this isn't how I visualized things going. We didn't find a dress, my makeup's not touched up, and I haven't practiced what I'm going to say."

"Leann, this is Lloyd we're talking about. You look great, but you could show up wearing a trash bag and he'd still be head over heels for you," Shay said. "Go get your man," she said, nudging me.

She was right. I looked down at the tattoo on my wrist. We were endgame. I was the queen to his king.

I waited for the pedestrian crossing signal to change so I could, as Shay put it, get my man. Then I saw her, and again I could not move. I knew Lloyd casually dated during our off-seasons, and so did I, but I had never been unfortunate enough to actually see it. He wasn't one for social media, so I never even saw him in pictures with other women when I'd try to stalk, er…, research his life without me.

Still, he couldn't be that serious about her. At least, not serious enough to pick her over me, I rationed. I took a deep breath and was about to cross the street when she turned and I saw her profile. I couldn't believe it. But, maybe she was just a coworker or a friend's wife, I hoped. Then Lloyd rubbed her tummy and gave her bump a kiss. A bump that looked to be about five months along and that Lloyd was laying claim to. My hopes were shattered.

I felt my legs turn to Jell-O, and I nearly collapsed. Gwen and Shay had apparently also noticed what I'd seen and were there to steady me.

She was pregnant – pregnant with Lloyd's child. There were no words for what I felt. Our breakup had broken my heart, but until now I thought the pieces could be put back together. Now, there were not even pieces left to mend. I was hollow inside. I just wanted to melt into the sidewalk and allow people to press their heels into me.

Nothing could hurt more. Then the pain turned to anger. *Why didn't he tell me?* I would have understood. No, I wouldn't have, and he knew that. We always said no one got us like we got each other, and this was no different. He still should have told me. Here he was living this double life, when it went without saying that we were endgame, that we were supposed to be the king and queen left standing victorious on the chessboard.

But now our bond was destroyed. He was no longer the person in which I had so much faith. The trust was gone. I felt as though I'd been too abruptly woken up from a dream that was now morphing into a nightmare.

Then, it dawned on me. Maybe, he didn't love me anymore. My mind was spinning as every belief I had about life and love was called into question. How could there be such a thing as soulmates? If love was supposedly indispensable, how could one's feelings be so interchangeable? Everything around me started to look so plastic, so unrealistic. I felt as though the sun would soon take its toll on these Mattel-made people. What was love? What was true? I could no longer visualize a happy ending.

I knew I should have moved. I'd been standing on the corner, staring at him for too long. It was only a matter of time before he turned his head and spotted me from the restaurant window. I kept trying to force my limbs to vacate the premises, but they would not budge.

As the tears started to accumulate, I felt it coming. Breaking from a succession of laughter, his eyes found mine.

My feet finally awoke. I jetted down the street before I could even see his reaction. Maybe it all happened fast enough that he didn't make out my face. As I ran, I felt a rush of adrenaline that I only otherwise felt in moments of motherhood – killing spiders with my bare hands, lifting couches to free my pliable child from his endless endeavors – that allowed me to continue sprinting several blocks until I reached the hotel.

As I fled, I recalled other times that I'd run from Lloyd – both in anger and in playfulness. There was not a single time that he didn't run after me and pull me into his strong embrace. I always felt protected – until now. I knew he wouldn't be following, and it was very unfamiliar territory.

I walked up the stone steps that led to the hotel entrance. I just wanted to shut my eyes, but I knew that shutting my eyes wouldn't shut off my thoughts. I begged my mind to give me a break because my heart could not handle it anymore. I didn't want to think, feel, know. When I made it into my hotel room and was finally out of sight from any prying eyes, I collapsed on the floor and really allowed myself to feel hurt and all the other emotions fighting to be released. Shay and Gwen made it back to the room about twenty minutes later and found me in the same spot on the floor, sobbing.

Shay laid there with me without saying a word. She just coexisted in a time that I needed her presence. A little while later, she prepared a bath and a glass of straight scotch. I sat in the tub until my skin faded to a stark white, pixelated color. I watched unresponsively as my phone moved across the rim of the bathtub with rhythmic vibrations.

I wasn't going to answer, but when it started to ring a third time curiosity overtook my hesitation. For a moment, I thought maybe it was Lloyd trying to tell me it had all been a big misunderstanding. Alas, it was my mother.

"How's the trip going, sweetie? You and Lloyd back to making lovey-dovey faces at each other?" she teased.

I didn't have the heart, or the strength for that matter, to tell her the truth.

"No, I haven't spoken to him yet. I'm still hanging with Shay and Gwen at the hotel."

I asked her to send me some pictures of Renz, hoping that would cheer me up. As she was relaying a story about his latest adventure at the playground, I got a text alert. Thinking it was the pictures from my mom, I opened the message without much thought.

The message was not from mom, however. It was from Lloyd. My heart sank. I came up with a quick excuse to get off of the phone with my mom. Then I paused, saying a silent prayer, before reading the text. I crossed my fingers that this was just a misunderstanding and hoped that I was about to read a message explaining that he had recently met a pregnant long-lost cousin or something.

Instead, the text read: "Meet me at our spot."

We had a special meeting spot on Pier 84 on the Hudson River in Manhattan's Hell's Kitchen neighborhood. In the past, I would be so eager to see Lloyd that I probably would have jumped out of the tub and ran out of the hotel half-dressed. This time, there was no endgame, so I was not compelled to move. I did not know if I could handle seeing him. An overpowering sense of hate for this man was beginning to build up inside of me. But a part of me still loved him. That part got me out of the tub. I had to hear what he had to say.

I rummaged through my suitcase in a lackadaisical manner then pulled out a sundress and threw it on. I let my damp hair stick to my back without even bothering with a comb. At this point, appearance was meaningless.

As I neared our spot, the remnants from the sunset faded away, and the fireworks began. I looked up at the sky and stared. But the beauty of the moment was lost on me. As I brought my head down slowly, I saw the ever-familiar silhouette of Lloyd approaching. As much as I wanted to just lash out at him, I was in a comatose-like state. The shock was still very overwhelming.

We were about seven feet away from each other when he stopped. He couldn't even look me in the eye. That hurt beyond words, and my eyes swelled up so fast that I was unable to make out his distinct features. I hated to let him see that this was breaking me, but I could not hide what I was feeling. The devastation shown clear through every part of my body no matter how hard I fought to hide the pain. As the tide in my eyes began to subside, I saw that he was on the verge of tearing up too.

My voice cracked as I pushed the words out of my mouth. "Do you love her?" As I heard the sentence aloud, I realized I didn't want to know the answer.

He grimaced and fought back the release of tears. His reaction said it all. My eyes sunk down as they often did when I could no longer handle my emotions. I kept searching his face, but I only had a side view. Then I asked "Do you still feel it?"

"Always," he said. "I always feel it with you. Even when we're apart, you're with me."

Those words brought tears to both of our eyes.

"I didn't think you could love anybody as much as you loved me," I responded.

Without hesitation, his eyes finally met mine as he said, "I never could. You know that. But this situation... I... I can't walk away from it."

I was so lost and confused. I knew in my heart this was our truth, but the fact that he hid something so important from me destroyed my intuition. Although he said he could never love another woman as he did me, there was an understood exception to this fact. It was something that would drive us apart, but also contribute ten times over to my love and respect for this man. The exception being children.

I never told Lloyd, but I admired him so much for the way he stepped up as a father figure to Renz. I would never ask or even want him to leave his child to have a life with me. Maybe we had our chance, and now it was just too late. Maybe this was the universe's way of letting us know that we were not meant to be, that we were not endgame after all.

I knew Lloyd's history with his father, and because of that history, I knew he would go above and beyond in fatherhood. As absolutely destroyed as I was, I was also very happy for him. It was a weird, bittersweet feeling. He should have been having children with me, but I never made a big enough sacrifice to make that possible for us. That was something I'd beat myself up about for a while, but I had to face reality.

We both stood there, emotions overflowing, the reflections of fireworks cast over our faces, for what seemed like an eternity. I turned away before letting myself completely melt down. I walked away quickly and headed back to the hotel.

I knew he couldn't come after me, but I sensed that he wanted to. I was on auto-pilot the rest of that night. I knew that first thing in the morning I would have to change my number.

♟♟

I chugged the last few swigs of Moscato straight from the bottle to get those bad memories out of my head. Letting the bubbly overpower my thought process, I reasoned that the best way to rid my mind of negative thoughts about Tavern Blue was to make new good memories there.

"Tavern Blue it is," I told Gwen. "We can both wear something from my closet," I said, motioning her towards my room.

I was ready in fifteen minutes, but Gwen looked me up and down and I could tell that she was not satisfied with my attire.

"Fine. Primp away," I said and took a seat on the edge of my bed.

Gwen's face lit up. "You still have that blue shimmery top and the leather skirt I let you borrow, right?" she asked as she made a beeline for the drawer she knew I put all the clothes and accessories she'd either left at my house after crashing from a night of bar hopping or let me borrow and never taken back.

She pulled out a tight red dress that she planned to wear and the blue top and black leather skirt for me. She then grabbed my makeup bag, turned on the radio and headed towards me.

"You look great, honey, but I'm just going to add a little more drama to your face. You ok with some fake eyelashes too?" she said.

Although she framed it as a question, I knew she wasn't really asking. I simply closed my eyes and let her do her magic.

Gwen was chatting away while she did my makeup, but

my attention had turned to a tune coming from the radio – "Say Something" by A Great Big World and Christina Aguilera. The lyrics took my mind back to Lloyd.

$$♟♟$$

After we'd parted ways at the pier three years ago, I returned to the hotel and threw myself the grandest of pity parties. Shay, the good friend that she was, had picked up ice cream and chocolate from the corner store while I was out, and Gwen had rushed to her apartment to bring her DVD player and a stack of comedies for us to binge watch.

Still, I spent much of the night crying despite the ladies' efforts at consoling me.

"You're looking a little, well, *Death Becomes Her*," Shay said, referencing the 1992 dark comedy we'd just watched.

"Really," I said, sniffling, "Madeline or Helen?"

"Definitely Madeline," Gwen piped in. "After she loses her color, minus the head twisted backwards of course."

"Of course," I said. "But, hey, I'll take a comparison to Meryl Streep as a compliment any day," I joked between sobs.

"On a serious note, are you ok?" Shay asked.

I took a deep breath and gave her a raw, honest answer. "No. But I will be."

It was not the first and would not be the last time life would disappoint me.

I thought back to when I caught Marc fooling around with a girl who had been a close friend of mine. I was eight months pregnant at the time and they had the audacity to go at it in my car. The pain from those circumstance was penetrating enough, but Marc – rather than apologize or try to make excuses – told me it was my fault for getting too fat.

"The kid's only like five pounds but you're packing at least fifty," he said.

Angry, humiliated and hopped up on pregnancy hormones, he got a swift jab to the jaw that busted his lip before I could rein myself in.

But I got through that moment and all the other crap Marc put me through. I'd get through this as well. I was a stronger person, thanks in part to Lloyd. Still, this was my time to wallow. The next day, I'd be on a flight home and would have to put on a happy face for Renz. Now was the time to get out all the tears rather than burden my eight-year-old with any signs of sadness and longing.

46

Shay practically read my mind. "You let it all out. You don't have Renz or anyone else to worry about tonight but yourself," she said, and put her arm around me so I could literally cry on her shoulder.

Shay always had my back, even when we were kids. Considering the way we met, she had every right to hate my guts but instead she chose to stand up for me. We were in fifth grade, and being the klutz that I am, I tripped over my own two feet walking down the hall. But as I was falling, I reached out trying to grab something to prevent me from hitting the floor and took down the girl beside me. That girl was Shay. The other kids started laughing, and I expected the gorgeous girl with long jet black hair and freckles that highlighted her fair skin to kick my butt, or at the very least start laughing at me as well. Instead, she stood up then reached her hand down to help me up.

"What are you laughing at, Tommy? This is nowhere near as funny as when you peed your pants at the museum field trip last year," she said, immediately bringing his laughter to a halt. She proceeded to riddle off a few more embarrassing mishaps about the kids still laughing until they all shut up and went on their way, having already mostly forgotten about my fall.

I could always count on her and now, as I struggled to get over Lloyd, was no exception.

The following day was dark and dreary as a summer thunderstorm was rolling in. The weather, I thought, was quite fitting given my mood. Shay and I said our goodbyes to Gwen then headed for the hotel lobby to grab a cab to the airport. We decided to leave extra early in case the storm affected our flight, and I couldn't wait to get out of the city.

As I handed the taxi driver my carry-on luggage, I almost didn't believe what I was seeing. Lloyd was on the other side of the street, dodging traffic to make it to me before I got into the cab.

I frantically searched his face. There were no words. Nothing could be spoken that wasn't already understood. We both knew this was goodbye, for good.

"I had to say goodbye," he said, a bit winded. "I couldn't just leave things… unsaid, unfinished."

Without thought or hesitation, I kissed him. I knew we were over. I knew he was spoken for. But I could not help it. Our last kiss had been seven months ago. I needed one more to remember him by. Apparently, so did he. When I tried to pull away, he tightened his embrace and refused to break the kiss.

"Ahem," Shay interrupted. "I'm sorry, but the cabbie's already started the meter. We've still got tons of time before our flight. I'll go now, and you stay and settle things with him," she said to me. "Lloyd, you make sure she makes it in time to the airport for our five o'clock flight," she said sternly to him.

"Will do," Lloyd said. With that, he grabbed my hand, and we headed to the subway to get to his apartment.

Closure. This would provide me closure, I told myself. We just needed to have a good, long talk so there were no unanswered questions or regrets about what we wished we had told each other. This way, we could both move on. I knew it would not change our circumstances. The truth was he had lost me, but I had to share the accountability. We lost each other.

But as we made our way through the busy streets and maneuvered through the crowds on the subway, I began to second guess myself. What was I doing? Why was I going to his apartment? Nothing could be said that would provide closure short of Lloyd professing his undying devotion to me and us riding off into the sunset. Part of me hoped Lloyd would sit me down on his couch and say he wanted to find a way for us to be together. But thinking this made me feel guilty and selfish. There was a baby on the way, and I needed to step aside.

With all these thoughts racing through my mind, we made it to Lloyd's place in no time. We had not spoken a word to each other during the commute, but had also never stopped clutching each other's hand.

He was still holding my hand as we sat down on his couch. I started to think that maybe my visualization would pan out better for me this time. We were, after all, on the couch. All he had to do now was profess his love. But then the inner turmoil started up again in my head, and I couldn't help but think that the happy ending I wanted would make me a homewrecker.

Lloyd was about to speak, but I excused myself to the restroom. I didn't know what I wanted him to say, but I knew I wasn't prepared for whatever he planned to get off his chest. I splashed some water in my face and looked at myself in the mirror. I was still a bit pale, my eyes were blotchy from all the crying and I had not a lick of makeup on. Unconsciously, I started trying to fix my hair and adjust my top to look more presentable. Then, it dawned on me that to him I was beautiful regardless. He once told me he loved my mind and wit more than anything that was merely skin deep. He also quipped that it helped that I had a great rack, knowing I would get his sense of humor, so I figured a little boob adjustment wouldn't hurt, especially since this was likely the last image of me I would be leaving with him.

I opened the door to the bathroom and stepped right into Lloyd's chest as he'd been waiting at the door. He put his arms around me to steady me. Then I made the biggest mistake. I looked up, and our eyes locked.

There were no smiles, no movements; our faces were raw and expressionless. I could feel his eyes piercing through mine as though he could see into me, like he was witnessing my heart spell out his name with each beat. Our eyes searched each other's faces as if we were taking mental photographs, something we could hold onto for years to come.

Neither of us wanted to forget this moment, or any fragment of the other's face for that matter. I wanted to capture every mark, scar, and dimple. I wanted to embed him into my long-term memory. As we studied each other, he placed his right hand on my cheek. My eyes closed as I savored his touch, and my mouth opened slightly as I took a deep breath in. I wanted to breathe in this air, the air that occupied this time and place. Maybe somehow I could breathe deep enough to hold this air inside of me forever.

We stood motionless for some time. Then he kissed me, softly but passionately.

There wasn't enough time to let the voices in my head have a cat fight. They could duke it out later as more important matters were at hand. Regardless of our situation, I could not bring myself to break away from him. I was getting on a plane in a few hours and would probably never see him again. I needed desperately to have one last fairytale moment, one last touch, one last taste.

I don't even remember how we ended up in his bedroom, with little to no words being spoken. We lay naked on his king-sized bed, surrounded by huge goose down pillows. The room was dark but glimmers of sunlight that shown through the curtains illuminated our bodies. We stared intently into each other's eyes, undistracted, as if a tethered rope was holding us together while we made love. I took his hand and placed it on my chest as I had done so many times before. His fingers found their way up to my mouth, and I savored his sweet skin, knowing this would be the last time. My hands grazed his arms, stroke after stroke, in an attempt to memorize his body.

Then his mouth began to explore, kissing my lips, my neck and down my arm. He nibbled at the tattoo on my wrist, the spot eternally reserved for him. Without warning, he lifted me off the bed and pinned me against the wall. My legs were wrapped tightly around him, relishing the feel of him. His pace quickened, but he remained in constant control, satisfying the needs of my yearning body. I didn't want to let go. Now or ever.

The intensity took me over as his lips made their way from my neck back to my mouth. Our tongues entangled as we both found our release. He gently lowered me back onto the bed and peppered my still writhing body with soft kisses. It had been the most beautiful, mind blowing, spiritual encounter we ever experienced. We lay wrapped in each other's arms and eventually dozed off.

I woke up an hour later and untangled our bodies, careful not to wake him. I looked back at my love as he slept. I knew that no other woman could ever see him in the same light that I did. I also knew the love we had could never be touched. But, I knew he would stand by the other woman to raise their child together. I had to let him go. After all, I had a kid of my own to get back to. I grabbed my shoes and clothes and left the apartment without a word. There was really nothing left to say.

For months after, everything reminded me of Lloyd. The pattern in my toast would resemble his profile, the radio host for the morning show I listened to would tell a joke that I was sure Lloyd would think was hilarious, and TV commercials were constantly referencing New York.

Shay forced me out on a couple of blind dates, stressing the adage that the best way to get over someone is to get under someone new. But none of the dates progressed to that level. I couldn't help but compare these men to Lloyd and none came close.

I spent my first New Years in six years without Lloyd. Even though I had a date, the kiss ringing in the new year was lacking. I started to worry that I would never feel with any other man the way I felt when I was with Lloyd. At only twenty-eight years old, it was a depressing thought that maybe I already had the love of my life and any future relationships would simply be lackluster.

♟♟

Gwen finally finished my makeup, I pulled myself out of depressing thoughts about the past and we made our way to Tavern Blue. As we waited in line outside to have our IDs checked, I took a moment to appreciate all the good memories I was lucky enough to have accumulated in New York. The Big Apple was my favorite place in the whole world. Of course, my worldview was limited, but as far as the span of my imagination could travel, New York was at the top of my list.

Throughout my involvement with Lloyd, I was able to travel to so many places and experience so many things – the West Coast, the Caribbean, even a few trips to London. For that, I was truly grateful. I couldn't help but smile as the neon blue lettering outside the club radiated off my face. I began to shiver. Partly because it was 35 degrees, and partly because I was nervous.

"Leann!" Matty, the door man, exclaimed. "Girl, give me a hug. I haven't seen you in ages," he said and scooped me up into his arms. Matty was a big guy. He had been a semi-pro football player before suffering a knee injury and boasted a good 300 pounds.

He and I went way back. I had been a regular at the club and we'd developed a friendship close enough that he once held my hair back after a few too many tequila shots when things with Lloyd were still new and I didn't want him to have such an unsavory image of me in his head. Matty was a big Italian guy. He was your typical New Yorker. Strong accent, short tempered, and smart mouthed. I adored him. Lloyd had gotten in so well with the club owners that we all used to stay after and do shots at the bar.

We would all crack on each other and sit up all night pondering the many mysteries of life, and glass garnishes. Matty was always taken aback by my quick wit and ability to roll with the punches. I was like one of the guys, just with great legs and a great ass, he used to joke.

"Hang around after closing and we'll catch up," he said.

He then escorted us inside to a table and comp'd us two bottles of champagne and instructed the cocktail waitress to cut the bill for whatever else we ordered in half. He also took my jacket, scarf, earmuffs, gloves, leg warmers – what can I say, I'm from Florida – and dropped them off at coat check.

"I have to get back to my post outside the club. You ladies enjoy yourself," Matty said.

"Thanks. I've missed coming here," I told him. Before he left, I whispered, "Have you seen or heard from Lloyd lately?"

"Not in a while."

Before I could dwell on that, Gwen yelled over the music, "You look hot, girl! Get that groove thing on the dance floor," she said, pulling me to the center of the club to dance.

Gwen was always the life of the party. She was in each and every way a true NYC girl. She came from money, and lots of it. Her parents owned a chain of insurance companies. Her father's cousin's family, were the owners of the St. John. Gwen had options. She would never be jobless.

Her first choice had been to work in the hotel. She wanted to be in the glitz and glam of the city. Truth be told, Gwen didn't have to work at all. She had a trust fund, but she wanted to earn her own way and had a very independent mindset. She managed the hotel and was quite good at it. The entire staff at the hotel was like family to her.

As we made our way to the bar, we ran into some familiar faces, including Gwen's cousin David. David always had a thing for me but never acted on it because of Lloyd. But according to Gwen, he would often ask her if we were hanging out without Lloyd whether we'd broken up, eager to scoop me up if I ever became a free woman. Now, I was single and ready to mingle. A group of us pounded back jaeger bombs and then retreated to the dance floor.

The liquor and the DJ had my adrenaline pumping. And David had managed to rev my hormones into high gear as he grinded behind me to the beat of the music. For a spoiled rich kid, he could dance. I attributed his rhythm to his mother being of Spanish descent.

We danced for hours without so much as breaking for air. As the club made its last call, David leaned in and kissed me. It could have been a beautiful moment, but I was haunted by the memories of all the kisses that took place in this very club between Lloyd and me.

I ran out the back door and almost got sick behind the club. Matty was there and made sure I was alright. Once the queasiness settled, he helped me back inside. He offered to take Gwen and me to a 24-hour diner to get some food to help soak up some of the liquor coursing through me.

We took him up on his offer, but not before I apologized to David for my abrupt reaction. He understood, and he gave our cab driver our fare for the ride to the diner. Gwen and I sat in a small booth side by side with Matty across from us. Gwen and I were both pretty buzzed and were cracking up as we re-capped the night. She and Matty found it hilarious the way I ran out on David. I was still mortified. Two omelets and a side of fries later, it was time to venture home.

I let Gwen crash at my place as I often did. I hated for her to travel the streets of New York so late at night. She had witnessed a stabbing on the subway when she was in her teens, and since then she would never ride them after sunset. I gave her some sweats to sleep in and we were both knocked out in no time.

CHAPTER FOUR

Pawns of Love

I could have let the fact that Lloyd did not reply destroy me. But, ironically, Lloyd had drilled into my head so many times that it was not ok to let a man dictate my happiness when we would discuss Marc and other not-so-stellar relationships from my past. The message stuck even if the man behind it did not. This too shall pass, I kept telling myself whenever the sting of Lloyd's apparent rejection (assuming he still had the same number) would start to overload my tear ducts.

Of course, that doesn't mean I didn't obsess over it just a little. For a month after I sent the text, friends and coworkers had to walk on eggshells with me regarding certain topics, namely relationships. I was either, let's say, overly emotional or downright snippy when the topic of love was brought up.

For instance, a Burger King commercial with a boy around Renz's age and his happy and in love parents brought me to tears one day. And I don't even root for BK. I'm a McDonald's chick. Still, something about the traditional, nuclear family smiling at each other over their growth hormone infested food made me weep.

On the other side of the spectrum, my manager one day kindly suggested that I go home and take a mental health day after I went on a tirade in response to one of the nursing home residents wheeling past me and asking, "Why aren't you married yet? A pretty little thing like you shouldn't be working behind a desk. I'll keep my eye open for a husband for you," she said and kept rolling.

I should have just laughed it off. But if a severely-staged dementia patient could tell I was a catch and show concern that no one had put a ring on it yet, why hadn't any of the men in my life? Unfortunately, I had this conversation out loud instead of in my head.

"You're right, Norma. Why am I not married?" I called after her. "I'm honest, trustworthy, caring, witty and have the looks to boot. Why hasn't anyone snatched me up and taken me off the market for good yet? Hell, I can't even get a guy, well, the guy to answer my damn text. What is wrong with men?"

At this point, Norma seemed to have forgotten her initial question to me, and I realized that I'd gotten a little too excited. Everyone in the back office could hear me, prompting the suggestion that I head home for the day. A bit embarrassed but still riled up, I took my manager up on that offer and went home.

A few other outbursts like that had my coworkers running for the hills anytime I'd step into the room while someone was discussing their significant other. I think some of the employees who didn't know me as well were convinced that I was hitting the bottle.

Luckily for everyone around me, my snark and drama over the unanswered text died down significantly as time passed.

By the time spring had arrived, it was pretty much a distant memory. Besides, I had more pressing concerns. Renz would be leaving to spend part of his summer vacation in Florida with his dad and visiting my family while he was there.

I was frantically making sure I knew everything there was to know about sending an unaccompanied minor on a flight. I'm sure the airline customer service representatives were getting tired of my twice daily phone calls, but when my child's safety was at issue, I didn't care if I was becoming a nuisance. The guilt was also pecking away at me that I would not be joining him on this trip. It would be his first time back to Florida since his grandmother died. At my core, I knew that I should have been going with him, but I wasn't ready yet to face my childhood home knowing that my mother would not be there.

June was here in no time, and the Saturday morning that Renz was to leave for Florida had come. Renz and I had packed his suitcase the night before, but I was suddenly struck with a fear that I was sending him off without something he would need. But what that something was had not become clear in my head, so I started throwing little extras into a carry-on bag: Q-tips, extra socks, Band-Aid's, fruit snacks, a flashlight, batteries, and other natural disaster supplies. What if Florida ran out of electricity? I had to account for everything. Good God, I was turning into… Cheryl. I tossed the bag aside and went to wake Renz up.

We had breakfast together, and I made sure Renz knew what to expect at the airport. The airline would grant me a security pass at the ticket counter so I could escort Renz through security and to the gate. I'd be able to stay with him at the gate until he boarded, but he'd be on his own from there. Of course, they'd introduce him to the flight attendant and he or she would be charged with making sure he was ok during the flight and getting him to Marc, who would be at the gate when he arrived.

I looked at the excitement on Renz's face and reined in my anxiety as I did not want my irrational fears to be projected onto him before he was about to leave. I put on a brave face and helped him with his luggage. Outside, I hailed a cab, and we headed to the airport.

As his flight boarded, it took everything I had to keep the tears in check until he could no longer see me at the gate. I was already missing him and could not help but worry that something would go wrong and I wouldn't be there to protect him. I knew his father would be there to meet him when he landed, but I still couldn't shake my misgivings about sending him alone. I thought about my idea to pack him a parachute and was kicking myself now for not going through with it.

Once his flight took off, I called Marc to make sure he had the right flight number and arrival time. I stressed to him the need to call me as soon as Renz landed to confirm that he was in one piece. He obliged and my tensions all faded away when I heard Renz's voice. He regaled me with a colorful albeit overly dramatic account of the flight and some of the other passengers.

When I woke up the next day, I had, for once, absolutely nothing to do. I looked over at my TV and could see myself getting sucked into mindless channel surfing for hours with nothing to watch but reruns and the same movies that had been playing all month. I decided the bookshelf in the living room was a better place to look for something to occupy my time.

I had a shelf where all the books I hadn't gotten around to reading yet ended up and would likely stay as I was sure to buy a new stack of novels to start before I caught up. I affectionately called these my friend-zone books - those that were great to have around in a group but would never make it to my bedroom. Perusing the shelf, *Pawns of Love* caught my eye. I had tried to start it once, but life got in the way, and I'd completely forgotten about it. I picked it up but then put it back. I remembered buying the book because the title, with its chess metaphor, made me think of Lloyd. I was hesitant to open that can of worms again. I kept looking on the shelf, but nothing intrigued me. There was a reason they'd been put on this shelf after all. What the hell, I said to myself, picking up *Pawns of Love* and heading back to my bedroom.

I snuggled under the covers, but before I could start reading, I saw that it was finally a decent enough hour that I could call to check in on Renz.

"Hey buddy. How's it going?" I asked after Marc gave Renz the phone.

"Great, Ma. But I gotta run. I have to fill my tackle box."

"Wait, what?"

"We're going fishing. And the early bird catches the worm so I gotta hurry and fill my tackle box with lures and stuff for fishing. So can I go, Mom?"

"Of course. Have fun. Let me talk to your dad."

I reminded Marc to make sure Renz wore a lifejacket if they were going out on a boat. We wrapped up the conversation pretty quickly after that. I was having a hard time picking my jaw off the floor. Marc fishing, and at seven in the morning? The thought was blowing my mind. Nonetheless, Renz was clearly having a great time and Marc was taking this time with his son seriously. This made me happy and helped put my mind at ease. Now, onto that book.

♟♟

The book began with "Chapter One: They Meet." I had assumed that L.L. Grellin was a woman because, well, most romance authors are women. But the protagonist of this story was a man on Spring Break in Cancun, leading me to believe that L.L. was also a man. There was no about the author page in the book to confirm my suspicions though. A few more pages in and I was really questioning whether my psyche could handle me reading any further. So much about the book reminded me of Lloyd, and I went a little haywire the last time Lloyd got stuck in my head.

The past months' events with Lloyd not answering my text simply had me projecting my situation onto this character, I told myself. The fact that the main character was on Spring Break, as I had been when I met Lloyd, was merely coincidence.

The writing style was compelling, and I already felt a connection to the male lead. That was probably why it was making me think of Lloyd. I couldn't fault a book for being authentic and written so well that it was already pulling at my heartstrings. No, this was a book I needed to keep reading.

As I walked past Tio's Bistro, my attention immediately went to one of the patrons sitting outside on the patio. Her hair, dark brown with blonde highlights, was eye-catching. Her skin looked as though it had been airbrushed with gold flakes. I couldn't take my eyes off of her. She was by far the most exquisite girl I'd seen since arriving in Mexico. I didn't care if she saw me gawking. I also couldn't just keep walking by without trying to make an impression on her as well.

"Hold up, fellas," I said. "Let's grab some tacos outta this joint."

Andre was quick to bust my balls. "Bruh, you hate tacos," he said.

That was true, but I had to play this off. "No, I hate that crap Pollo Loco serves by your house. This is that authentic shit. Get your game up."

That made me laugh out loud. Lloyd confessed to me after we'd been dating awhile that he hated Greek food. The only reason he'd come into the Greek place in Daytona was to get my attention.

We got a table, and I ordered a meal I had no intentions of eating to give myself time to come up with a game plan for getting her digits. Then I saw her walk in and take a seat at the bar. She was looking around like she was trying to find someone. I knew now was the time to make my move since she was away from her friends. I got up from the table and made my way just a few feet behind her. I still didn't know what I was going to say, so I hesitated. This girl had guys swarming her since I saw her though she seemed not to notice. I would have to come correct if I wanted to not end up like all the other guys she'd blown off.

Shit, she was getting up to take her margarita and shots outside to the patio, and I still didn't know what to say. To hell with it, I couldn't just let her leave. I'd just have to wing it.

I headed towards her, but a few drunk frat boys started a shoving match. One guy got pushed right into her, sending her flying forward. In those shoes, there was no way she was going to regain her balance. I had to act fast.

Luckily, I made it just in time to catch her. Unfortunately, I also caught the remnants of her drinks all over my pants.

What the fuck?! My mind was in overdrive. This had gone way past coincidental. Who was this L.L.?

I flipped the book to the dedication page. "To the one that got away," it read. I then sifted through the pages to glean the different chapter headings. "Empire State of Mind," "Stepson," "Club Aqua," "Baby Mama," "The Break Turned Breakup." My eyes skimmed bits of each chapter. There was no doubt in my mind. This was our story. And though the places and names had been changed, there was so much detail that I knew Lloyd had to have been the one to write it. There was no way a family member or even our closest confidantes would know this much about us.

I couldn't believe it. I sat motionless, in shock, for at least five minutes straight. I didn't know what to do. My first instinct was to flip to the end of the book and see how the story ends, but I resisted that urge. I knew Lloyd better than anyone and I knew he didn't want me to cheat. I had to read our story, cover to cover, out of respect for him. I went into the kitchen and took a few swigs of wine. It was five o'clock somewhere, and this situation was more than deserving of a mood stabilizer. I then settled with the book on the couch.

I clutched it between my hands, wary of what I would find inside. These were Lloyd's inner thoughts about our relationship. What if I was wrong, and he didn't want me to read it? This was the equivalent of reading someone's diary. Me finding the book was a one in a million chance. Maybe he wrote it as a therapeutic exercise, thinking I'd never see it. After all, he didn't tell me about it. What if reading it was a violation of his privacy?

I didn't know what to do. My natural reaction, in situations like these, was to call my mother. But reality quickly sunk in. Unless I planned on having a séance, she wasn't going to be able to give me any answers. Not having her guidance during such a monumental moment like this made my heart feel shallow, and I began to cry.

I couldn't help but flashback to all the instances that I would just pick up my phone and text my mother. Her reassurance, her vibe, her understanding - I could no longer feel any of it and that made me feel utterly alone. I tried to think about what she would do and say in this moment. As I longed for the nurturing wisdom of my mother, I reflected on all the years I had been blessed with it. I still could not believe she was gone.

♟♟

Her troubles began late in March last year. I was planning a trip with my parents to Orlando to take Renz to Disney World and stopped by their house to go over the details. I let myself in and headed straight to the computer to rummage through hotel rates while Renz went to play video games. My mother hadn't been feeling well earlier in the week, but I thought nothing of it. She peered over my shoulder to tell me how ridiculously overpriced resorts had become and then went upstairs to take a shower. Forty minutes passed, and she still hadn't come back downstairs, so I went up to tell her we were all booked. I was surprised to hear the water still running in the shower. My mother was not one for lengthy showers as an advocate for water conservation, an issue we butted head over often when I was a teenager.

"Ma, are you almost done? I want to go over the itinerary with you."

There was no response.

"Mom," I said more loudly, thinking she couldn't hear me over the flowing water. "Mom, can you hear me? Mom!"

Still no response. I was getting worried now. "Mom, I'm coming in."

I took a deep breath as I opened the door, praying that she just had water in her ears but preparing myself for something horrible. And horrible is what I got. She was slumped face down on top of the shower curtain that had detached from the rod and fallen to the floor. I gently turned her over.

"Mom, can you hear me?" I said in a panic. But she still did not answer. She was breathing, as I could see her chest moving up and down, but her breaths were shallow and she was so pale that it looked like all life had been drained out of her. My phone was in my pocket. I pulled it out and called 911, and they directed me to do CPR until a paramedic arrived. I covered my mom in her robe and started CPR.

60

"Mom, what's going on?" I could hear Renz calling as he made his way upstairs.

He must have heard my cries. I didn't want him to see this. Seeing his grandmother like this could traumatize him. Shoot, it was traumatizing me.

"I'll be right back," I told my mom. I rushed to the top of the stairs and cut Renz off. "Grandma is really sick. I need you to wait for the ambulance downstairs and let the paramedics in when they get here," I told him.

"What's wrong my grandma?" he said. He looked terrified.

"I'm taking care of her, and I need to get back in there with her. I need you to be brave, ok? Let the paramedics in. Grandma is counting on us," I said then kissed the top of his head. "Now go," I said, motioning for him to go downstairs.

He rushed back downstairs. "Don't worry, Grandma. I'm brave. I'll let the ambulance in," he yelled back.

I hurried back to my mother and continued CPR. The paramedics were there quickly and got her loaded into the ambulance. Renz and I following behind in my car. While in the car, I called my father who was at work and told him what happened. He said he'd meet us at the hospital.

Mom was alive, but the doctors informed us that she had a severe stroke. The left side of her face was droopy and her body was hunched to the left. She was lethargic, slurring her words and not able to finish her sentences. The doctor said she had a complete loss of motor function on her left side. I was devastated.

That night, I tried to keep it together as I consoled my son as he wept relentlessly. As his tears soaked my shirt, I cradled him and tried to conceal my own tears as much as possible. He finally fell asleep, and I gave myself just five minutes to break down. I could not dwell in sorrow. There was work to be done. Mom would need long-term care, and I was determined to get her into the nursing facility where I worked. I started making calls to get her a bed.

Later that night, when my phone started ringing, I thought it was going to be Beth, the intake director at the nursing home, to update me on the availability of a room for my mom at the facility. I answered without looking at the caller ID. To my dismay, it was the hospital.

They told me my mother's condition had taken a turn for the worst. Her heart stopped. They were able to resuscitate her, but her blood pressure was increasing rapidly and would likely cause another heart attack. In her weakened state from the stroke, they were worried that they would not be able to get her back again when that happened. My father was by her side, having never left the hospital. He had asked the nurse to call me so Renz and I could come back and say our goodbyes before it was too late.

My world was collapsing around me. I couldn't see through the tears and I could barely breathe with this weight on top of me. I felt empty. Then, anger took over. I screamed and punched my bedroom door. I was furious. It wasn't just that I was about to lose my mother, but that I had to tell my child. I never in my life felt more helpless than at that moment.

I thought for sure my scream would have woken Renz up, but he lay so peacefully, unharmed by the news I had just received. I was about to turn his whole life's happiness upside down. I sobbed violently into my hands. I then touched him tenderly. I knew we were running out of time. All that I could force out of my mouth was, "Come on, honey, we have to go to the hospital."

He was half asleep and probably thought it was morning. I put a coat over his pajamas and helped him into his sneakers. We were well on our way in the car before he really came to and asked me what was going on. It was in that instant I knew I could no longer protect my son from the harsh realities of this world. I could no longer reassure him that everything would be okay, as my mother always had done for me.

I told him grandma was getting worse, and we needed to go see her. My heart sunk as his facial expression changed. We were both silent for the rest of the drive, full of anxiety, full of heartache, and in complete despair.

I couldn't believe this was happening. We were supposed to be going to Disney World. Instead, we'd be planning a funeral. I couldn't imagine my life without my mother's presence, without her embrace. I couldn't imagine my young son having to deal with such a powerful loss. I just wanted to give up, to sink into my seat and just stop breathing.

As we neared the hospital entrance, I saw my father waiting for us. I stopped the car and let Renz out to go to my dad while I went to find a parking spot. I caught my reflection in the rear-view mirror and looked at a face that I knew would not smile again for a very long time.

Once I made it into the hospital, I took the elevator up to the floor my mother was being cared for on. When the elevator doors glided open, I saw my entire family in hysterics in the hallway.

Stone faced, I sprinted towards my mother's room. Nurses were unplugging her monitors, and they all looked at me as if to say, "Sorry." They may have been "sorry," but this wasn't their mother. They didn't care; they didn't hurt. I hated every person in that room that still had a mother to hug, call, argue with.

I walked out of the room stoic-like and touched my son's hand as he lay coddled in my father's arms. My brother sat against the wall of the hallway, face in hands. His wife huddled my two nephews to console them. I blankly walked into the stairwell. I couldn't breathe again. As the door shut behind me, I collapsed. I cried so hard I thought I would hyperventilate. How did this happen? How could I go on? How could I mother my child when I was now a shell of a person?

My mother took care of me. She laughed with me, cried with me, and advised me. She told me everything would be okay when I couldn't see the silver lining. Now she was gone. I was suffocating in my own tears. I didn't want anyone to console me. All I wanted was for my mother to come into the stairwell, wrap her arms around me, and tell me everything would be ok. Never again would I have that relief.

That night, we all stayed at my parent's house. It was silent, no one spoke a word. It wasn't one of those "oh, great uncle Henry died, let's all talk about his quirks" type of losses. She wasn't supposed to go, ever in my mind. Everyone sat around sobbing all night. I heard my father go upstairs, scream, and then punch something. Then, he came back down to be in our presence. No one wanted to go upstairs.

I had been staring at the same spot on the wall for hours, helpless to do anything else, when the sun rose. My son was still asleep in my arms, and his cousins were also snoozing in the warm embrace of their mother and father.

The next couple of days leading up to the funeral were a fog. I hated everyone. I knew I was supposed to be strong, but in my mind I said fuck that and fuck all of you. I did, however, have extra affection for my son. But whenever I'd try to hug him, he'd just fall into a heart breaking hiccup of cries.

The funeral was held at my parent's church. It was beautiful but, honestly, I can't recall much of what was said because it was all so surreal. I was well aware of the hundreds of flowers and the revolving door of attendees that sincerely looked broken up over my mother's passing. Friends and family showed up from up north, down south, out east, and everywhere else. There were people she had worked with at different jobs, and those she helped out in the community. Even people from the local businesses she frequented, such as the grocery store, the bakery, the flower shop, and the hardware store, came to show their respects. I could not believe how many people kept showing up. People I hadn't seen since childhood, and even people I had never seen before. She made such an impact, but again all I kept thinking was you people probably still have your mothers. I was angry, but at the same time I was proud of her for the profound impact she made on so many lives.

As I peered over at some childhood friends, I thought of how my mother was always the one they gravitated to when they needed an adult's help but weren't ready to confide in their own parents yet. My friends could talk to her about any and everything. I couldn't be so selfish. Others were grieving as well. I looked next to me at my son and noticed him praying. I knew he was talking to her. I felt a smile dawn my face for the first time since I'd found her in the bathroom. I didn't know how it emerged, but it was nice to know I still was capable of producing one.

Moments later, my son stood up at the altar. He was compelled to say something, so I encouraged him, nodding my approval.

"My grandmother was a beautiful, amazing woman. I'm very lucky to have had her as a grandmother, and I'm glad that you all got to experience her greatness too. We are all so lucky," he said, managing to hold back sobs until he'd returned to the pew with me.

I looked at my son with such admiration, this little boy was so much wiser than I. He saw the beauty in everything while I was sitting back dwelling on the misery. He made me so proud, and I knew he was the product of not only me but of my mother's influence as well.

I could not shake my sorrow though to be a bigger person. At the end of the funeral, when everyone was hugging and consoling each other, I didn't want anyone to touch me. Out of respect, I played my role and shook hands and said thank you to those offering their condolences.

I could not wait to be alone, so I could explode. My family had rented out a hall where we would celebrate the life of my mother. As I fixed my son a plate of food, I methodically dropped it off to the table he was at with his cousins. I then acted as if I was going to the bathroom and slipped out the side door. Shoes in hand, cigarette in mouth, I inhaled the outside air.

Then, I looked to the sky and in a flood of tears whispered, "Why did you leave me?" I was talking to my mother, but I was also questioning Lloyd. Why had he taken the route he chose, leaving me to endure this pain all alone? I hated him so much for not being there.

I had noticed my sister-in-law wiping tears from my brother's face, and I wished I hadn't been so hesitant to get back in the dating game after Lloyd. There had been some casual dates but nothing ever got serious enough for me to have someone by my side, being strong for me, on a day like this.

My heart went out to my father who was also alone now. Like my son had said, he was lucky. He spent more than thirty-five years with the love of his life. At that moment, I made a conscious decision to stop holding onto my past. I would live my life for my son and me. I was sure this was how my mother would want me to live. She would often tell me to get out and meet someone, but my rebuttal had always been "they're not him." I knew it was time for me to heal in more ways than one.

That night after the funeral, I felt so empty. But I guess I preferred feeling empty over feeling pain. My parents' house filled with people. People from our past and present. People offering condolences. Yet, all the while I was thinking "your comfort does nothing, you are not MY mother." I was dead inside. I wandered upstairs where I found my brother's best childhood friend admiring a picture of my mother that hung on the wall.

He said without looking up, "You know, she was like a mother to me." Bret had lost his mother at a very young age so he had always looked to my mother for that unconditional bond. I smiled meekly and then slipped away into my parents' bedroom.

It was there I could finally find solace. I wanted to sleep, but I knew when I woke up there would be that split second where I didn't recall the heartache and pain, and then I would be bombarded with it all over again. I kept myself awake for as long as I could. I planned out the future for my son and me in that one night. I decided we would move, start over. I had some money saved for a rainy day, who knew it would be a tsunami. The school year would be over for Renz in about three months, and that's when I would get us out of here, away from all the heart wrenching memories.

♟♟

Wiping tears from my face, I snapped out of my somber mood

and decided I was going to read this book. If Lloyd didn't want me to read it, then that was just too damn bad. He shouldn't have put our story down for millions to read and expect me to be the only one not to get any insight from his words.

Lloyd and Leann had become Ace and Arianna in *Pawns of Love*. I thought it was cute that he kept the matching initials. The story continued to the night we kissed at the beach bar.

> I saw Arianna across the bar taking 'em back like a champ. Nothing turned me on more than a woman who could hold her liquor. She was no doubt the most beautiful woman I had ever come across. It wasn't her obvious outer beauty that intrigued me. It was her quirks and eccentricities that kept my attention.

His words took me back to those moments. I recalled being self-conscious about the skimpy cover-up I had been wearing over my bikini. I thought it made my breasts look lopsided, and the girls were still recovering from the full year I put them through breastfeeding.

> She had on a halter dress with a flower pattern. It reminded me of something you'd see in a gift shop while visiting a tropical island. She looked gorgeous, but I could tell she was second-guessing her choice of attire. She kept adjusting her boobs in the dress although I wasn't sure whether she was worried that she was showing too much or not enough.
>
> Every time she thought no one was looking, she'd make an adjustment to her rack and then scan the bar nervously to make sure no one had seen her. I was cracking up inside but did not want to embarrass her. I had not made my move yet, and she didn't know I was watching her from across the room. I thought her failed attempt at discretion was adorable.

As I read that I started laughing. I had no idea he had seen me at the bar or at any point before we united on the dance floor.

> I decided not to approach her right away. I thought we had hit it off at Tio's Bistro, but I was not sure if she had felt the same connection that I had. After all, she didn't give me her number at the end of the night. But her friend did arrange for us to meet again, so I was hoping the minor diss of not sharing her number was just part of a hard-to-get front she put up and

not a true blow-off.

Besides, guys had been approaching her left and right, and I wanted to observe her reactions. As beautiful as she was, she seemed a little stuck up. Having given guys dirty looks and snarls since she took her seat at the bar, I was almost intimidated to approach her. But I was too cocky and enamored by her to let that get in the way.

As I watched her shoo away the flies, I planned out my move. I started to head towards her, but then she looked in my direction and I panicked and turned away. Real smooth, I thought to myself. Before I could attempt another play, she disappeared onto the beach. I followed, keeping my distance, admiring her beauty from afar. She literally took my breath away.

I continued to watch her when she made her way back into the bar. She seemed to be looking for someone. For a moment, my ego had me convinced she was trying to find me, but then I realized it was far more likely that she was looking for her friends. Once she spotted them, she continued to look around and seemed disappointed.

I smiled at the thought that maybe she was looking for me. To hell with wondering, it was time to make my move. Plus, if I didn't make my presence known soon, I was coming dangerously close to straddling that line between good-hearted admirer and creepy stalker.

I figured a bold gesture was best. I walked up behind her and wrapped my arms around her. The moment I touched her, I felt sparks going off throughout my body. I had never felt such a strong connection to someone so fast.

For a woman that was used to expelling men, and one whom had played so hard to get, I never expected her to spin around and kiss me. It went without saying that our instant chemistry was not just a figment of my imagination but something she was feeling as well.

Not to brag but having a beautiful woman on my arm for the night was not a new or rare occurrence for me, but something stood out about Arianna. It was the first time in a long time I didn't just want to smash. We spent the rest of the night laid up on the beach, talking. Just talking, like some high schoolers. I told her things about my life, upbringing, and aspirations that I hadn't even shared with my closest friends. I don't know why I instantly felt so comfortable around her and eager to open up. But we were building a connection, a bond that night that could not be tethered.

The next day, I convinced Arianna to come jet skiing with me. She was not by any means the submissive type and insisted on getting her own jet ski rather than riding with me.

I was used to chicks that would let me lead and play their part, but this one was as hard headed as me. It intrigued me. I could tell she had no clue what she was doing, but she faked the hell out of it. I liked that she was trying to impress me. Still, I had to annihilate her in a race. Unfortunately, trying to keep up, she took a turn too sharp and went smack into the water. She cussed me out afterwards, and I offered to take her to grab a bite to make it up to her.

It was so out of character for me to be wining and dining a girl I'd just met, with no ulterior motive. I usually just left a trail of breadcrumbs, and they'd follow suit. On top of that, I was agreeing to things I'd never consider with anyone else - like eating oysters. We'd slipped into a seafood place, and when Arianna ordered oysters for us to share, instead of declining because I generally was appalled by slimy creatures, I was going head to head in an oyster eating contest. Arianna and tequila had me doing things I'd never do. I didn't want to admit it to myself, but I had already fallen in love. We went shot for shot, Corona for Corona, oyster for oyster. Before I knew it, we were taking body shots, just the two of us in the middle of the restaurant. Neither of us even questioned where our friends were, we were so morphed into each other.

Further, being with Arianna was like being with one of the guys. I didn't have to censor myself around her. When my friends joined us, after our extra public display of affection at the seafood restaurant, and made plans to go to a strip club, she was on board. What's more, she was throwing dollars and slapping asses right alongside of us. The sun had risen and set, and we were still intoxicated with each other. That night we went from hotel to hotel, partying like teenagers. I felt young, I felt alive, and I didn't have a care in the world. One hotel we entered was having a wedding reception. We crashed the party and took over the dance floor. I must say her moves were tantalizing. I wanted her, right then and there, in front of everyone.

I pulled her close to me, and we just gazed at each other as if to say, "I know you feel this too." We slow danced, to fast music. It was like me and her were the only two people in the banquet hall. As her head lay upon my chest, I lifted her chin to look into her eyes once more. Then, I kissed her. It was a kiss that I wanted to last forever. She had me. We both knew that in a couple more days we'd be going our separate ways. We held each other tight and savored this moment in time, the only one that we were guaranteed.

The next day while we relaxed in a private cabana, we talked about the future. Everything was moving so fast, but in my heart I knew I couldn't let this girl go. She lived in South Carolina, and I lived in Florida. She was also a single mother and would never think of relocating because she had a support system for her child where she was. I was overly consumed with my business and wouldn't relocate either. It was going to be tough, but we were determined to continue seeing each other.

That night, our friends insisted that we dish on what was going on between us. Her friends, being typical females, were very skeptical of who was occupying all of their girl's time. My boys were only worried about if I was smashing. Unfortunately, I wasn't. This girl had taken up my whole vacation, and I wasn't even getting any. Yet, I didn't care. A guy could never admit this though to his boys. So, instead, I did the typical male ritual of grunting and slapping hands, insinuating but not admitting to anything.

Although I wasn't getting any, our friends sure as hell were hooking up. Sometime around 3 am, someone suggested that we go skinny dipping, and no one was sober enough to object.

At first, the idea sounded hot. Naked women with water dripping from their beautiful bodies was the makings of any man's fantasy. But then the realization that my friends would be checking out Arianna's goodies before I even had a chance to do so began to gnaw at me.

Luckily, only two of my boys had jumped into the water with their asses out before we saw police sirens and made a run for it. Only later did we notice that the cops were breaking up a bar fight and had not even noticed us. But the moment had passed, and no one felt like returning to the water. Instead, we went to the girls' hotel room, ordered room service, and popped open a few more beers.

All of us were drunk out of our minds, and yet again someone had another brilliant idea, this time to play spin the bottle. Liz, Arianna's best friend, landed the bottle on Ari. They kissed, quickly and innocently, but still drew hoots and hollers from the fellas. Then, Ari was up to spin. As the bottle started to slow, I noticed it was about to land on my boy Jake. Before it did, Ari took the bottle and pointed it at me.

I didn't hesitate to draw her into a deep, passionate kiss, which prompted cheers and a bunch of commotion from our friends. They taunted us, asking if they'd be in the wedding. We just laughed. I knew I was going to get shit from the guys for my unbreakable attraction to Ari, but I didn't care. I was infatuated with her.

The following night would be my last in Cancun. My balls were as blue as the resort pool, and I wanted Ari more than anything. We had talked about keeping in touch once we both ventured home, which I was onboard for, but I knew that if I didn't close the deal before leaving, there was a chance I never would. I feared that once she got back to her regularly-scheduled programming, she would forget about me.

On that last night in Mexico, we didn't sleep. But not for the reason I was hoping. I pulled out my best game that night, but Ari quickly called me out for fronting and not being real. She wanted to know that this attraction, this connection was real. She said she didn't just want to be a notch on my belt. If things were meant to be, she said we'd find our way back to each other.

She seemed to have a thing for tempting fate. I was still getting to know her, but it seemed like something or someone had damaged her in the past. And now, she couldn't accept anything at face value. She had to keep testing my feelings for her and true intentions. But I was up for the challenge. A girl like this, and the instant connection we had, did not come along all the time, and I knew I had to see this through. If she needed me to wait and prove myself to her before she could truly trust and let me in, I would show her I was the real deal.

That night we stayed up talking — and making out — but mostly talking. I'm a smart man, but Ari had a way with words that captivated me and made my mind look at things in new ways. She was also clever and had me agreeing with shit that I didn't even know I was agreeing to. Her beauty, her intelligence, her humor, I could never understand how one woman could have it all.

When the time came to say our goodbyes, I kissed her forehead and told her I'd marry her one day. I don't think she knew how much I meant that. I was never the type to believe in love at first sight, soulmates or any of that TV romance, mythical shit. But Ari had me rethinking my beliefs. Watching her leave that morning sent a wave of knots through my stomach. I had no idea any woman could make me feel that way, especially in such a short time.

My thoughts were scattered post-Mexico. Ari was front and center in my mind and was crowding everything else out. Anytime I saw a Mexican restaurant, I would remember our first encounter. If I saw a funny commercial on TV, I wondered what quip Ari would have made about it. When I passed a jewelry store, I had to avert my eyes and pick up my pace to prevent myself from doing something crazy like buying a statement necklace or opulent earrings to send to her.

I couldn't even focus on my work. As a talent agent for a small company, I was often tasked with selecting models for different ad campaigns. Whenever a fresh face would come into my building, I was quick to see a flaw in them, for not exuding the same level of perfection that was apparent in Ari's beauty.

We kept to our word and stayed in touch after leaving Cancun. I'd find myself checking my phone, turning it on and off to make sure I didn't miss a text from her due to bad reception. It was almost embarrassing how hooked this chick had me.

My coworkers had a running joke at this point about me laughing at my lap because I couldn't control myself from breaking into hysterics anytime I got a funny or sarcastic text from Ari.

I never felt as connected to anyone as I did to Ari. She got me in ways that nobody else could. I'll be the first to admit I had many flings and was the type to never go to bed alone on the weekend, but all that lost its luster once I met her. I found myself comparing everyone to her, and of course no one could compare. Some girls had the looks, but no brains. Some had the humor, but not that perfect body type. And even those that had beauty and smarts didn't have that dimple that fit around the right corner of her lip, and they couldn't match that expression she would make when she was mad that was just too animated to take seriously. They just weren't her.

After months of late-night phone conversations, pondering life's most important questions, discussing chess strategies and trying to figure out the origin of words like 'fork' and 'spoof,' we made plans to see each other again. She was going to drive out to see me because I was backed up with work and my schedule wasn't as flexible. I remember literally jumping when she said she would come. I spent a good seven days rearranging and cleaning my place. By cleaning, I mean hiding shit under the rug, but the effort was made.

I felt like a restless child on Christmas Eve the night before her arrival. I stared at my table tops making sure my bachelor décor would be appeasing to her. I caught myself thinking, "Will she like the bulldog paperweight, or is it too much?" After going back and forth staring at this damn paperweight, I finally stuffed it in a drawer. I just wanted to impress her and surely a bulldog paperweight wouldn't be up to par for a girl of her stature. I opted to let my Maxim subscriptions adorn the table rather than the paperweight.

Then, I made my way to the fridge and started disposing of anything that looked past its expiration — so basically everything. All that was left was soy sauce and Guinness, but it beat moldy cheese. I meticulously placed the bottles of beer in the fridge drawer and got rid of the box that they had once resided in. Boxes aren't classy, I thought to myself. As I made my way to the bedroom, I was sure to Febreeze the carpets and comforter. After all my hard labor, I couldn't sleep. I could not wait to smell her lavender scented hair and caress her cocoa butter drenched skin.

Approximately eighteen hours later, she called to tell me she was getting off at my exit. I waited impatiently for her to pull up. I had this thing about wanting to see her before she saw me. My nerves were shot, and I didn't want her to see me so, well, chick-like. As she pulled into my driveway, the anticipation couldn't be any more prevalent. The driver's door swung open, and I saw a suede blue heel plop out onto the pavement. One thing about this woman was that she could dress. I knew her friends kept forcing her into skimpy outfits to hit the town each night in Cancun. Don't get me wrong, I loved the look, but her style during the day was conservative by comparison yet very chic and put together. She wasn't flashy, but she tended to do one statement piece. Today it was those suede blue heels.

She stepped out of her car, and I could see her lips were shimmering with gloss and her skin was as sun-kissed as ever. A gust of wind suddenly swept her beautifully highlighted hair across her face. This seemed to frazzle her. She actually thought it was possible that I might be dissatisfied with her appearance.

This girl had no clue how beautiful she truly was.

She used the side-view mirror to examine her tresses and put each lock back in place. Just as she finished, a ball rolled past her and into the street with a kid chasing not far behind. She stood in his path and although I couldn't hear their conversation, I presume she told him not to get near the street and promised to retrieve his ball. She jetted from her car, across the street and back before any cars could damage the ball, and returned it to the elated child. Back beside her car, she caught a glimpse of herself in the mirror and started the effort to fix her hair all over again. It was in that moment that I knew I loved this woman.

Seeing her struggle with her luggage took me out of my trance, and I ran out to help her. When she saw me, she dropped everything in hand, ran up to me and wrapped her arms around me ever so tightly. I could feel an overwhelming calm enter my body. Arianna fit so perfectly in my arms it was as if we were designed for each other. Her smile stretched ear to ear, showing off her accentuated cheekbones.

"I missed you, my chipmunk," I said, tightening my embrace.

"I told you to never stop believing in magic," she responded.

Arianna had this zest about her, she was very free spirited and believed in the unimaginable. Fairytales were not something I had a lot of experience with, growing up in the streets. It amused me to see this light in her eyes whenever she'd talk about happy endings though. I always joked about how the only happy endings I'd receive would be from a chick named Jin Su, to which she would always roll her eyes, not appreciating my humor while she was trying to be serious about fairytales. The irony was not lost on us.

"You still believe in that crap, Ari?"

"If anything, I believe in magic even more now that I've met you. You don't feel this, Ace?" she questioned, putting her hand up against mine, fingertip to fingertip.

Like clockwork I felt what could only be described as butterflies racing through her hands to mine. Electricity, chemistry, magic - I didn't know what to call it but it was real.

But as chills circulated throughout my body, I just looked at her and grinned.

"Nah, I feel a hand. You're crazy, baby. Unicorns and wizards, nobody's got time for all that," I quipped, not wanting to show all my cards.

As tough as I played it on the outside, I had a very romantic side. I planned on taking Ari out for sushi and then making love to her by candlelight. Apparently, she had other plans because not two seconds into the doorway, she started tearing off my clothes. When I say tearing, I mean she damn near ripped my t-shirt, trying to get it off of me.

Wait a minute, I said to myself. I wasn't that damn forward our first time, was I? I laughed at myself and then I blushed as I read more, reliving that intimate moment now through his eyes.

I picked her short ass up and threw her on my couch, and the adrenaline led us both into an animalistic trance. I unbuttoned her black tight shorts with my teeth and ripped them off before she could blink. I pulled her panties to the side and pulled her legs over my shoulders. She let out a growl as I teased her, and we both laughed in amusement.

I slid my fingers, now drenched in her wetness, into her mouth so she could taste what was now mine. Her eyes seduced me. She had so much sensuality, so much passion, that all I could do was nod.

She let out a gasp when my dick entered her, which only fueled my excitement. I couldn't help but feel a connection I had never felt before. I wanted to tell her I loved her right then and there, but instead I picked her up and stepped our carnal antics into high gear. I told her to fuck me like she loved me, and she went hard.

CHAPTER FIVE

Chess

I continued reading about our exploits during that trip. He had captured a moment in our lives that had been filled with pure bliss. At first, I worried that reliving these moments might turn melancholy, knowing that this man was no longer part of my life, and from the lack of response to my text, no longer wanted to be in my life. But instead, I felt honored to have known someone who truly made me happy, even if it was only for a brief time.

I could now think about Lloyd without just thinking about the bad, the end. We had so many good memories together. And, well, the sex was mind blowing. I wondered if he had included a particular early encounter between us that I was especially fond of. I kept reading and to my delight he had captured it in the pages of *Pawns of Love*. With nothing on my to-do list for today, I decided to indulge and read on.

On the beach that night, we were like teenagers, unable to keep our hormones in check. The scene was perfect with the sun setting behind our tangled silhouettes. We traced our names in the damp sand with our toes and accented the writing with an oddly shaped heart. We decided to spice things up and get a room right there on the beach.

Ari was very creative and suggested we roleplay. So we split up with a plan to meet at the hotel bar in forty-five minutes. The plot, as devised by her, cast me as a married man from Moscow away on business who finds himself in the presence of an alluring spy trying to infiltrate the Kremlin. She would seduce me and blackmail me into becoming her informant.

As I sat at the bar, I put my gullible face on. I had never roleplayed with a girl before, but Ari had this way of making me do things out of the ordinary. I was determined to outshine her at her own game. We were both very competitive and Ari could hold her own in most of the competitions we engaged in, but I'd surely get a Golden Globe before her.

She slipped up next to me in a pair of dark shades and a black trench coat. The determination on her face killed me. I wanted to burst out laughing but the more serious she took this, the more serious I got. Keeping a straight face was the hardest part.

"Are you alone, or is this seat taken?" she asked in a thick accent.

I simply motioned for her to take the seat. Then she said, "A fine-looking gentleman like yourself shouldn't be drinking alone. Tell me, are you in town for business or pleasure?"

"I'm here for business, and I'm alone at the bar because the wife is back in Mother Russia," I responded with an accent that I thought was fair game although it could have been English, Spanish or maybe even a tinge of Irish.

"Well, there is nothing wrong with mixing business with pleasure," she said, placing her hand on my thigh and leaning in closer to me.

It wasn't until then that I noticed she had sketched a Marilyn Monroe-type beauty mark above her lip. I couldn't help but smirk, but then it was back to my poker face. I was amused with her dedication to the part. She slid her room key in my hand, gave me a wink and left the bar.

I finished my drink and paid the bartender, then made my way to the hotel elevators. As each floor number lit up, I got more and more excited about my destination. The elevator finally arrived at the eleventh floor and I eagerly slam dunked my cardboard key into room 1122.

There she was, sprawled out across the bed with corset lingerie that had those little strappy pieces which attached to her knee-high stockings. My heart pounded, I was naturally attracted to her, but throw in the accent and I was a goner.

I went to pounce on her, but she stopped me. She had questions and wanted answers. Her dedication to this game started to annoy me at this point as I was ready to get to business, but she was so adamant about making me an informant. Rather than risk spoiling the mood, I presented her with a winner takes all proposition. I had noticed a chess board in the living room area of our suite.

"One game of chess, winner gets their demands," I explained. I wasn't surprised when she obliged since her competitive nature was almost as strong as mine.

For the next few hours, I taught Ari the game of chess. Of course, I quickly obliterated her in the first match. What could I say, the Russian business executive found himself with the upper hand over the spy and had a few aforementioned demands that needed satisfying.

But afterwards, I shared with Ari the art of the game of chess. It was a game that sort of set the tone in my life. I felt a man should always have a plan, and he should always be three moves ahead of the game in his head. There's a strategy, a technique, an intelligence that comes with chess. There's also the belief that the queen should always protect her king. I didn't expect Ari to pick up on it so quickly, but she did. I still won every match, of course, but she was good.

It was this particular night that my admiration for Ari grew drastically. Granted, we had impeccable chemistry and our attraction for each other was pure magnetism, but to be able to stimulate each other intellectually was another realm of attraction that I had never had as strongly as I did with her.

We spent hours upon hours talking about life's mysteries and our own particular beliefs. This stimulation of the minds naturally led to stirrings elsewhere, and we found ourselves on the balcony, under the stars, enraptured in passion.

When Ari's visit was coming to an end, I started to feel sick. I couldn't for the life of me understand why she had such a powerful effect on me. In my line of work, I encountered beautiful women on a daily basis, and I had developed several relationships throughout the years, but not one of them had an impact on me as great as Ari did. I decided on our last night together, I'd cook for her to show her my appreciation for her.

It was a three course meal. The lobster bisque, to start, featured a creamy sherry sauce, and the flavor exploded in your mouth. Each bite accounted for a new tasty sensation. The prime rib I prepared was just as exquisite, and the twice-baked potatoes were accented perfectly with pieces of chives. I could tell Ari had never had a meal this good in her life.

By the time we finished dessert, a molten chocolate cake, she couldn't stop praising me. She told me she didn't want me to lift another finger and began clearing the table. As she started to fill the sink, I turned her around briskly and just stared at her intently. My eyes searched her face and then I moved in slowly to taste her lips. I wanted to tell her I loved her, but I held back. Instead, I told her how much I was going to miss her and a tear escaped her hazel eyes. The innocence on her face captivated me. I knew parting this time would be harder than ever.

I knew this part of the book was supposed to be sad with my visit coming to an end, but I was in hysterics. Lloyd and cooking were two things that rarely went well together. He certainly took creative license in his description of the meal. He did cook, but that meal was a far cry from the one he depicted for readers.

Lloyd was a talented man in many arenas but cooking was not one of them. If a meal he laid out was exquisite, it was because he had ordered in. So, the meal he prepared for us before I had to return home from that first visit with him consisted of burgers and fries, which he somehow managed to burn.

But it was heartwarming to know that he challenged himself to cook to show me how much he cared. Although in reality all he could muster up was very, very well done burgers and extra, extra crispy fries, I was pleased to know that he thought I was a lobster bisque and prime rib kind of girl. Even though it was a seemingly small revelation, it pulled at my heart and sent tears down my eyes, but they were happy tears.

CHAPTER SIX

Revelations

L ittle did I know, bigger revelations were to come to light as I read further. But those insights would have to wait because Renz was calling. I had managed to call Marc about seventeen or so times while reading *Pawns of Love* to check in on my boy, but his phone kept going to voicemail. A part of me knew he was fine, fishing with his dad, but another part of me worried that maybe a whale had made it to the Florida shores and capsized their boat and my little man was treading water in the deep blue.

"Ma, relax, everything's fine," Renz said.

Annoyance protruded from his voice as, I guess, he saw all the missed calls on his dad's cell, which were probably closer to thirty-something than seventeen. Sure, I was paranoid and a little persistent at times, but his father's track record was far from flawless, and I was worried about my baby.

Renz kept insisting that he was having the time of his life, but then he caught me off guard. "I want to go to grandma's grave site. Dad says it will give me closure."

Dad says? Since when did he become so intuitive? I knew Renz had not wanted to go to the gravesite without me because he felt it would be too hard. I also didn't want him to have to face those emotions alone but could never quite bring myself to go.

"Ma? What do you think?"

I didn't know how to respond, so I told him we should talk about it later. My heart raced at the thought of visiting the heap of dirt that was my mother's final resting place. It was marked with a cold stone that read "Beloved wife, mother, grandmother." Those words weren't enough to depict this perfect human being, this indescribable character that was her. Those words were too general. Everyone's a mother, a grandmother, a third cousin, a stepson. Simple nouns that could describe anyone were all that was left of her.

I ended the call somewhat uneasy. Renz's request was just too much for me to handle right now. I decided to jump back into my past. At least my mother was alive inside *Pawns of Love*.

> Ari was coming down for another visit, but this one would be different. This time she was bringing her son. I had to admit I was nervous to meet him. I wanted him to like me and didn't see any reason that he wouldn't, but kids are fickle. I stuffed my pants with candies but quickly removed them after my coworkers told me I looked like Petey the Pedophile. It was obvious I had no idea what I was getting myself into.
>
> Even though Ari and I steered clear of "future" conversations we both knew we were each other's happily ever after. I wanted to be as much of a father to Jacob as I could be since his father had passed away.

I had to stop and snicker after reading that. It was so like Lloyd to just kill off Marc, and I loved it. Not that I'd wish any ill will on Marc, but he put me through the wringer so I didn't mind a rendition of my story that did not include him.

> If anyone could understand how important it was for a boy to have a strong father figure, it was me. My father's absence while I was growing up really took a toll on me. I remembered the day he left like it was yesterday. At the time, I was living in New York City. I was six years old, and I just hopped on the city bus home from 42nd Street right outside of my elementary school. I would always ride the bus home with an older woman who lived in my building and got off work from the nearby bodega at the same time school let out. It's something my mom had arranged since she was terrified of me roaming the city alone.
>
> My teacher Miss Peterson had allowed us to make

something out of wooden popsicle sticks that day, and I was eager to get home and show off my finished piece. It was a crown. When Miss Peterson asked me what the crown meant to me, I told her it was the king's job to take care of all his people just like it was the father's job to take care of his family. I explained to her that my pop liked to use chess references to teach me what he called life lessons. He taught me about the importance of a King ruling his castle. I was so eager to get home and give it to him.

As the bus came to a stop, I rushed up to the door before the driver could even open it.

"Boy, you better slow down," Mrs. Linder, the woman in my building, urged behind me.

I fell through the door and picked myself up to run up to the third level of my building. As I ran to my door, the number 305 got larger and larger. I busted through my apartment screaming "Pop, Pop!"

I hadn't even noticed my mother because her flannel PJs acted as camouflage on our couch. The blinds were shut tightly and the front room was so dark, I couldn't really make out anything.

"Ya daddy don't live here anymore," she said somberly.

"What do you mean, Ma?"

"You heard me. He does not live here anymore, and he won't be coming back."

I looked at her stoic face and knew not to pursue the issue any further. I dropped my hand down that held the crown and marched to my room. I didn't fully grasp the magnitude of what she had said. I only knew he wouldn't be there anytime soon to marvel at the crown I made for him, and I was disappointed. It took a few weeks before it truly set in that he gone, and I was not going to see him again. When I lost hope that he would come for me, I buried that crown behind our building right beside the swing set my father would often take me on.

For years, I resented my mother. I blamed her for my father's departure and I hated her for it. In grade school, I would still talk about him as if he still lived with us. When friends would come over to play, I would just say he was out of town on business. One year, I followed through with the guise that he was an astronaut. He could be any hero I wanted him to be through lies.

When I was around fifteen, I found out the truth about

my father. He was selling drugs, running the streets, hooking up with any and every one. He wound up getting, as was described to me, a rich chick pregnant and wanted to leave our family to be with her. I guess the woman had given him an ultimatum along with promises of financial security, so he chose her.

What got me the most was that all of my memories of my father were good ones. How could I not see the narcissist that he was? I respected the fact that my mother protected me from the painful details for all the years and regretted holding it against her. To imagine the amount of pain she must have gritted her teeth through just to be strong for me is heart wrenching. She loved me and made so many sacrifices for me, and my inability to do the same left me with so much guilt after her passing.

I remember the pure look of empathy on Ari's face when I told her about my childhood. She understood how important it was for me to be the man that my father couldn't be.

We spent countless hours talking about the imaginary brood of kids we'd have - enough to field a football team, or at least the offensive line - and the family rituals we would embark upon. Of course, no plans were ever made. Neither of us would talk about relocating. We just envisioned an end where we would somehow meet. After meeting Jacob, I knew I would have to accomplish something big in order for our pieces as a whole to fit.

Jacob was three years old when I first met him. They came by plane because the car ride would have been too much for him. I was there to meet them when they got off the plane, dinosaur in hand. Jacob had a thing for dinosaurs at the time. When they first approached me, Jacob kept putting his head on Ari's shoulder. He was acting very shy, far from the precocious toddler I'd heard all about. Then, I showed him the green pterodactyl, and he gasped in excitement. He reached for me and from then on we were inseparable. Ari was a bit jealous that he preferred me that whole weekend, but I loved to feel needed. No matter how much a mother provides for her son, there is still a dire need for a male figure in a boy's life.

This became glaringly clear during one particular outing at an outdoor burger joint for dinner when Jacob started throwing a fit. Ari had warned me that he kept throwing tantrums at home and she could never calm him down. Time out was like a field trip to him, and her scolding just made him laugh. As Ari started to panic in embarrassment, I took her hand and smiled. I talked to Jacob in a firm voice and took away his dinosaur. I told him he couldn't have it back until he behaved. Now I'm not saying I'm the baby whisperer but, yeah, that's pretty much what I'm saying.

I think Jacob just needed a stern man-to-man talk about appropriate dinner behavior and what was not allowed while out in public. I could tell Ari was impressed by how well I had handled that and Jacob's receptiveness to what I had to say. I knew I wanted children and soon. As cocky thoughts of being the ultimate discipliner raced through my mind, Jacob shot me in the forehead with a spoonful of mac and cheese, but that's neither here nor there.

Despite having Jacob around, this weekend visit was just as fulfilling as our other rendezvous. In the absence of unbridled passion, there was commitment. In the absence of desire, there was loyalty. Instead of rolling around in the sheets, I was crawling around on the floor with Jacob. I loved it in its entirety.

The minute they got on their plane to head home, I was looking up real estate in South Carolina. My company was up-and-coming so I knew it wouldn't be possible to branch off and open another branch until this one was running itself. I could, however, plant the seed, get some property and rent it out until I was able to make such a huge move. It was a process that would take longer than expected.

Six months passed, and I was still searching. It was a plan in motion and it was meant to be a surprise, but Ari and I had started fighting. She had no idea that there was a plan in the works to get us closer together. Long-distance relationships aren't easy, even for people who spent years together before having to set out in different directions. And long-distance was all we had ever known, and there was no set date for the proximity problem to cease and no easy fix to remove the obstacles that stood between us. I could tell Ari was getting frustrated and wanted me to just throw caution to the wind and relocate to South Carolina. I knew not to expect such an extreme gesture from her as she had to put her kid first, so an impromptu move to Miami with no support system for her toddler was not in the cards for her.

But I couldn't just up and leave everything either. My father was a horrible role model, but his lessons about the King taking care of his kingdom stuck with me. I couldn't just move in with

Ari with no plan, no income, no prospects. She didn't take that into consideration when we'd argue, and I was starting to feel unappreciated and repelled by her spoiled nature. I loved the girl but I couldn't just leave everything I knew at the drop of a dime. I didn't expect that of her, and she shouldn't have put that pressure on me.

Our arguments started to put a strain on our relationship. True characteristics started to shine through, and I was mad that she wasn't willing to make the same sacrifices that I was already planning to make. I stopped searching for real estate and stopped talking to Ari.

My jaw dropped as I finished the page. I had no idea Lloyd was ever planning to move. Why didn't he just tell me? Then, I grew angry at myself. If I hadn't been so nagging, if I hadn't been oblivious to his inner turmoil, if I hadn't been such a selfish bitch. The what-ifs flooded my mind. Then, I remembered what came next.

I was in New York for business and I couldn't stop thinking about Ari. Our bond had turned into a love-hate situation. A part of me wanted to drown her, and the other part of me wanted to resuscitate her because I'd miss her too much if she were ever truly gone. How could she be so inconsiderate? After all the arguing, she hadn't even tried to make up with me. No calls, no singing telegrams, nothing.

I definitely wouldn't be the first to contact her no matter how much it killed me, but being in New York made that harder. The Big Apple had become an escape from reality for both of us. Every so often, I'd fly her out when I was there on business and we would roam the streets like tourists.

I felt so alone on this trip. I kept seeing things that would remind me of her. In Times Square, I noticed the Michael Jackson impersonator we'd always horse around with. I thought about the time she said she would moonwalk away from arguments if she knew how, and I laughed to myself. I took a picture of him to send to her, but remembered we weren't talking.

After a beer from the Irish pub that sat adjacent to my hotel, I made my way back to the hotel lobby. I never made it to the elevator bank because Danielle, the front desk clerk, and several other hotel workers that I had hung out and partied with on different occasions bombarded me.

"We have to go to the Empire State Building. They're doing a tribute," several people told me at once.

"A what?" I asked. It was obvious to me that something was up. No one was giving me straight answers, and no one seemed to know what the hell they were talking about. But I had nowhere else to be, they were always a fun crowd to hang with, and I could use the distraction from pining over Ari. "Fuck it," I said. "Let's go to the Empire State Building!"

"Woo hoo!" everyone cheered and continued their rowdy and possibly inebriated shenanigans.

Standing in line, I could smell the scent of fresh paint. They must have been remodeling a bit, and I was so fascinated by the simple architecture. Everyone was still eager to get me to the top to see some skyline tribute show. The elevator doors opened, and I edged my way out to the roof. Grabbing onto the bars, I imagined what would happen if I dropped a nickel.

I peered out to the brightly lit city and thought I saw Ari's profile in the patterns. Before I could turn around to question the tribute thing, I felt these little arms wrap around me. I could smell the cocoa butter and passion perfume that I had grown to love.

"I love you," she uttered, almost as if she didn't mean to but just couldn't keep those words bottled in any longer.

"I've always loved you," I exclaimed.

While this trip started as one of the loneliest I'd ever taken to the city, it would end with Ari and I stronger and more bound to each other than ever. We decided to get matching tattoos to symbolize our love. Sitting at the tattoo parlor, we couldn't decide what to get. She suggested A's for our names. I suggested the infinity sign to represent an unbreakable bond. We joked about his and her tats and how far we'd get in life. Then Ari came across something in the tattoo book that we both knew suited us best. The King and Queen chess pieces would be etched onto our wrists forever.

I went first because she was afraid I was going to chicken out last minute. I'd always had a low tolerance for pain and tattoos weren't necessarily my thing. She held my hand and laughed in amusement at my nervousness.

When she was up, I went to grab her hand, but she gave me a shooing motion and said "I got this." I couldn't clown on her cockiness; it was a result of my own. I put my hands up to surrender and watched as she was tickled with the tattoo gun.

Looking around the room at the discretely pierced tattoo artist's work, I noticed a piece that appeared to be the man's mother tattooed on his chest. I thought back to when I lost my mother.

I was only nineteen when she died and I had not yet come into my own. I had plans to go to college, but the subsequent events that caused my mother to pass altered my plans to even proceed in life. My mother who had never taken a cab a day in her life had gotten into a car accident the one day she decided to.

I was meeting with a scout from a prestigious New Jersey college to go over a scholarship offer. I played basketball all throughout middle and high school, and I was pretty good. Good enough to get offers for a four year ride to a few decent colleges.

I wanted my mother to be a part of my decision, so I kept urging her to leave work early that day but she told me it wasn't possible. She wanted to make it so badly that she not only left early against her boss' wishes, but took a cab in an effort to be on time. I got the phone call that she died on the scene and I collapsed.

For so many years, I resented my mother and now all that animosity went towards my father. The king was supposed to protect his people, a father his family. If he had done his duty, she wouldn't have been working three jobs to keep up with the bills.

But if I hadn't pressured her to come to the meeting with the scout, she wouldn't have gotten in that cab. My aunt had come to stay with me to help out with the apartment, but I had to get a job at the corner store on top of my job at a restaurant bussing tables. I didn't want to do anything. I started drinking heavily, trying to get out from under the guilt I felt over my mother's death and the years of resentment that I wrongfully directed toward her. She did so much for me, but I was blinded by the gold pedestal I had my father on for so many years. I recalled at the age of nine telling my mother it was her fault daddy left. If she had kept herself more attractive, he would have stayed. I said this to my mother as she showcased a stained blouse that had become stained from preparing my food, a burn on her hand that she accumulated ironing my pants, and a sweat-drenched forehead from the hard work she put forth while carrying the burden of being a single parent.

The memories haunted me, and I didn't want to go on. I spent endless nights under a bridge, drinking, self-sabotaging my future. It wasn't until years later that I really got my shit together. I had worked at a music store and made some connections over time with some C-list celebrities. Enough networking opened a door for me in Miami. There was really nothing tying me to New York anyway, with no family to speak of. I needed a fresh start. I wanted to excel in life and make my mother proud, so I headed to Florida with a partner to start up a promotion company.

Ari let out a yelp that brought me back to reality.

"What's the matter, tough girl? You can't take the pain?" I teased.

She flipped me off, and I laughed in amusement. It wasn't uncommon for me to zone out and reflect on the history with my parents. Most women I dated would often accuse me of thinking of another woman when I spaced liked that. It was true; I was thinking of another woman, but not in the manner that they accused. I would get lost in a mindset that no one could counter until Ari.

She was the only woman that knew how to find me, no matter where I would go mentally. Knowing her truly made me a better man. I remember one night she found me sitting in the bathtub, fully clothed, tequila in hand. She didn't say a word. She just removed the alcohol from my hand and climbed in with me. Laying her head on my chest, she knew that I just needed her. Soon my reckless, misguided efforts to find the unconditional love and compassion that a mother provided were eliminated as Ari met those needs.

After getting our tattoos, we went back to my hotel. That night when we made love, it was different. It was always passionate and the love between us seeped through our pores, but now that we had expressed it verbally and permanently symbolized it on our bodies, we could let our inhibitions run wild. As our bodies morphed into one, I felt intoxicated from the emotions.

Caught up in the moment, I inhaled her breath as if I was digesting her soul. We both just shook our heads in awe of something that was beyond us. This woman was undoubtedly my soul mate and only someone of her caliber could ever get me to fathom, let alone believe in, such a concept. I was a non-believer of such fantastical ideologies until her. No one could understand how you could love a person so much unless you had experienced it. We climaxed at the same time and without hesitation she pulled me deeper in that moment. That moment spoke volumes without the utterance of words, an unspoken truth that showed we were ready to take the next step in our relationship. We never spoke about that moment nor did a pregnancy result from it, but that moment of passion said that we had the same outcome in mind.

We were, as I liked to put it, endgame. We'd be the last pieces on the board after all the pawns and obstacles had been captured and faded away. I had no doubt we'd be old and gray, triumphantly yelling checkmate as we sat side by side in rocking chairs on the porch of our family home.

After this trip, I knew things would be different, and for a long time they were. The fighting subsided. We both knew a life without each other was not an option. My plan to relocate was back in motion, but I knew it was going to take some time. I started theoretically making chess moves so that my pawns would be in a row when the time came to strike.

But my intention to look for work in South Carolina rather than the much bigger and more obvious choice of expansion to New York did not sit well with my business partner Max Sidwell.

Max was a Bronx native, so he carried around a tough exterior and sort of untouchable attitude. He was 6'3" and 230 pounds with red hair. He was adamant about being a ginger Italian, but I never cared to question him. After years of partnering together, I felt as though I could trust him. Our five-year plan included him running our present company, while I ventured out to the root of it all, New York, to open up a secondary shop. We had started in Florida because we had formed connections and, as first timers, we wanted to form that foundation.

We were now over five years into our investment, and needless to say the Florida building was running pretty smoothly. We did promotional work, we advertised, we represented undiscovered talents. One of our clients had made it big due to our representation, and it was in our contract that Max and I would get equal percentages.

But after the last New York trip I had with Ari, Max felt that she was becoming a distraction from our goals and, honesty, it was true. I was searching for a location in the Carolinas instead of New York as we planned. But I reasoned that we weren't ready for New York.

Max could not disagree more, and tensions mounted as we could not find common ground. Our work environment felt as though a chalk line had been sketched through the office, separating us. The arguments were extremely unprofessional, and it was wearing on our routine. He finally agreed on me venturing off to the Carolinas, but insisted that I come up with some numbers on market value for that area. This would be the beginning to the end of a once great partnership. Looking back, I had to take full responsibility for how things played out, but I don't regret it one bit.

Having lived through extreme losses, I wasn't willing to lose the only person left who had a hold on my heart. I was willing to fight any battle, jump any hurdle. Whatever it took, I wasn't going to let anything stand in my way. At least, nothing that I could control.

Ironically, as things between Max and I started to fall apart, the bond between Ari and I was stronger than ever. I had a big meeting in New York to go over my South Carolina project, and she was meeting me out there with her son. He was now six years old, and Ari wanted to get him into show business. I was apprehensive to the idea, but since Jacob vocalized his wants to do so I obliged. I set up a meeting with the manager of a children's clothing line to see if Jacob could showcase his way in.

I was friendly with the manager, so Jacob was pretty much a shoe-in. When the time came to bring Jacob to meet Stanley Childs, founder of Zeek magazine, I had a decision to make. A text came in at the same time we approached Stanley's headquarters. The message was from Max. He had flown in to try to make amends. The message entailed a meeting that would be taking place in the next hour. If I wanted to move forward as partners, I would be there. If not, he would know my decision.

I knew going my own way would throw a monkey wrench in my South Carolina plans, likely leading to more delay. I looked Jacob in the eyes and asked him if he was sure he wanted to pursue this or if it was like the time he wanted to be a basketball playing astronaut. He was sure, which made me sure.

I deleted the text message and continued on to see Stanley. Jacob worked effortlessly at showing his charisma. The meeting was over in ten minutes, and Jacob was signed to do a cover for a children's clothing catalogue.

We let Ari believe the meeting was still going on while I took Jacob around Manhattan. We went to a museum, Madison Square Garden, and a donut shop where I was friends with the owner. Jacob was able to see how the donuts were made and assisted in the process. I took him on a horse and carriage ride through Central Park after that. Needless to say, out of all the culture I tried to embed in him, in one day, his favorite part was the guy dressed as Elmo wandering Times Square.

While we sat and had a slice of pizza for lunch, I told Jacob that even though I wasn't his real dad, I would always be there for him and take care of him.

My heart melted when he responded, "Is it ok that I love you like a real dad?"

I smiled and told him I loved him too. A few months later his modeling aspirations subsided, and he wanted to be a fireman. Again, I had no regrets.

Ari never quite understood why my business partnership ended. I went from being highly successful to just a step above living paycheck to paycheck as I ventured into a solo endeavor with a much smaller clientele. To keep those clients that I had left, I had to put in a lot more hours and do a lot more hand holding and coddling.

My diminished availability and constant need to meet clients' needs no matter the time or day irked Ari, who grew suspicious that all the added attention I was giving to work was being pointed at someone, rather than something. I caught her a few times checking my texts and call log when she thought I wasn't looking to verify that I'd been talking to a client and not just some female. But I had nothing to hide.

Although I had hooked up with models I booked for clients' events in the past, that was no longer the case and hadn't been since Ari and I got serious. Somewhere along our relationship, I stopped even looking at other women. They weren't my Ari, and they could never live up to her. Their eyebrows wouldn't turn in when they were angry the way that hers would, and they wouldn't bite their bottom lip when they were nervous as she did. They couldn't make me lose my breath in laughter over the stupidest shit like she could. Even if they could do all of these things, the truth was they just weren't Ari so I wouldn't have noticed.

Still, I was keeping my finances and business dealings private because I didn't want her to worry or ever think that she and Jacob were becoming a burden on me and a jinx to my success. I didn't want her to feel like any of what was going on was her fault. She had become so supportive of everything I set my sights on, and I just didn't want to disappoint her. What had started off as a surprise had turned into such a mess. I just wanted to be a man and get myself out of it on my own. I wanted to be successful and find a way to capture our dreams together.

However, my waning success started to wear on our relationship. Not only were her suspicions of my infidelity increasing, but financially I wasn't able to see her as often. The distance was once again putting a strain on our relationship. I started to resent her, mistreat her even. I was internally blaming her for the decline in my work. It wasn't her fault, she had no idea what was even going on. I couldn't give her answers. It was easier for me to project my feelings of inadequacy into anger, and unfortunately Ari was too often the recipient. I felt like a failure, and it became easier for me to put the blame on others than to take accountability for my actions.

On top of that, I started drinking heavily again. My demons reared their head, and guilt once again consumed me. I was mad at myself for failing and for taking my anger out on Ari. I felt as though I wasn't playing my part as a man, as her king. I decided then and there that Ari deserved better. But I couldn't give it to her, so I gave her space.

Months went by and neither of us tried to contact each other. Both stubborn as ever, but my firmness didn't stem from thinking I was right. It was the opposite. I knew I was wrong. She shouldn't have to bear the burden of my lack of success. I wanted her to prosper. I didn't want to hold her or her son back with any stress that I might provide. Letting her go was the hardest thing I ever had to do, but I guess in the back of my mind I expected to regain my success and win back my girl. I worked tirelessly at taking back control of my life.

I don't even know when I started crying, but my eyes were splotchy and red when I finished that chapter. Lloyd chose not to include my outburst at the Tavern Blue in his rendition of our breakup, either to not make me look bad or to spare himself from having to relive it. But the emotions he was dealing with were right here in front of me, and I had no clue at the time about how much he had sacrificed already and how much inner turmoil he was combatting.

Even before Tavern Blue, Lloyd and I had been fighting a lot. The distance between us took its toll on me and my constant need for reassurance pushed him away. I'm a woman of many questions, and I had admittedly pestered him a lot. I felt his feelings were changing, and I needed answers. *Did he still love me? Was his heart still mine? Was I depriving myself of the innate needs we have as humans while he was off being a playboy?*

Lloyd had jokingly referred to me as The Riddler, and even sent me a velvet green jacket with purple question marks sewn all over it. I didn't think it was funny. Normally, he and I would crack up to the point of mild seizing together. But my patience was wearing thin, and he knew it. I had sacrificed a lot to make our union work from afar. I just wanted the same sacrifices in return. I had no idea that he was making compromises and risking his career for me in an effort to close the distance between us.

I could have made things better. I wished he would have let me in. Things could have turned out so differently. But I knew Lloyd, so I knew why he didn't speak up. He was so stuck in that belief of being the king, the protector, the archetypal man of the house, that he would never share anything he viewed as a personal shortcoming with me.

To think, he was struggling to make ends meet and figure out a way to relocate while I was nagging and questioning his loyalty and fidelity. I failed at being his queen.

CHAPTER SEVEN

Moving On

I had to get out of the house and clear my head. I figured a stroll around Central Park would do me good. I got dressed, grabbed my purse and headed out the door. Two minutes later, I ran back into the house, grabbed *Pawns of Love*, shoved it in my purse, then made my way out again. The book was my own little piece of Lloyd. Now that I had him back in my life, I wasn't ready to be separated from him.

I strolled around Conservatory Water, more commonly referred to as Model Boat Pond, where locals came to show off their model boats and others rented one and navigated the waters, imagining they were on the high seas. The serenity calmed my nerves and took my mind off of what could have been with Lloyd and what Renz was asking of me now, as I let myself get lost in watching the little toy boats sail around the pond.

When watching the kids at the pond started to tug at my heartstrings a bit too much with Renz so far away, I started walking again and found myself at Bethesda Terrace. Lloyd had once told me this was considered the heart of Central Park.

I took a seat on the fountain and breathed in the fresh, crisp air coming off of the lake. I basked in the afternoon sun and took in the majestic grand staircases leading to the upper level of the terrace, with their mustard-olive colored carved stone and granite steps.

I remembered Lloyd telling me about the fountain sculpture, a bronze winged angel with four little cherubs beneath her that people called the Angel of the Waters. Lloyd said she blessed the waters and gave it healing powers. I was certainly in need of healing.

With the angel looking over me, I figured this was the ideal spot to delve back into *Pawns of Love*. I hoped she would give me strength as I knew the story only went downhill from here, at least for me. I hoped it would have a happy ending for Lloyd, even though I was not a part of it.

Boy was I right about needing strength from the angel and her cherubs. A few pages in and I saw a name I never expected to see, a name I didn't know Lloyd was even aware of: Graham Rell. Lloyd didn't even bother to change his name in the book. Considering what he'd done, I figured Lloyd was willing to take the risk of a possible defamation of character lawsuit if Graham ever found out he was called out in a book. I'm sure he also figured the risk was small because, well, Graham with a romance novel was an unlikely combination.

Seeing his name in print almost induced me to vomit, but more disturbing than remembering our relationship was that Lloyd knew about this guy. We started dating a few months after the blowup at the Tavern Blue. Come to think about it, my relationship with Graham probably started around the same time Lloyd started seeing his mystery woman, given how far along she was when I saw her. But I still had no idea how or why he made it into Lloyd's book.

Graham was a few years younger than me and was working as a personal trainer at the local college's gym. I was auditing a few English and creative writing classes at the university and would often frequent that gym - don't judge me, a single mom can't waste money on a fancy gym membership - where I'd often run into Graham, who everyone called Ham. I know, the name was cheesier than a number four at Taco Bell, and I should have known better.

But innocent flirting eventually blossomed into a full- blown relationship. I thought back to what led me into the arms of Ham to begin with. I'd have to blame it on a mix of missing Lloyd and reverting back to some of my old behaviors that were spurred by subconscious feelings of being unwanted.

With the mother I had, it's crazy to think that I ever felt unloved as a child but I lacked a strong connection to a male figure.

My brother and father were around, but they were not by any means close to me. I remember admiring and even being jealous of the father-daughter relationships depicted on TV and the real life close bonds I saw that my friends had with their siblings.

This dynamic in my home caused me to instinctively seek that nuclear family elsewhere. In high school, I rebelled and linked up with a group that was not so cookie-cutter. I felt accepted by them. I felt an unconditional love from them that I had been seeking from my own family. In my teens years, I quickly turned to drugs and sex to fill whatever voids needed mending in my psyche. However, I had this uncanny habit of going after boys who were incapable of making me feel loved. I guess a part of me was clinging to and was reassured by those feelings of apathy that I encountered at home from my brother and dad. At least that's what my psych professor embedded in me in college - something about self-efficacy.

Ham was my apparent temporary regression back into those patterns. He was so sweet at first, but I'd soon realize it was all a facade. I regretted not appreciating the pure and genuine love that Lloyd sheltered me with. We all had our imperfections, but Lloyd's were minute in the broad spectrum of things. Retrospect was becoming more and more painful.

Anyway, one rainy day I sat in my car debating whether I'd even attend class that day. Engine still running, my windshield wipers started fusing with the song on the radio. I decided I'd go to the gym instead. It wasn't uncommon for me to find any excuse to work on my fitness. It was too rainy to walk a few feet to class, yet not too rainy to walk the quarter mile from the only vacant parking spot to the gym.

I took one step into the air conditioned facility in my drenched clothes and chills immediately ran through my body and my teeth started to chatter. There was Ham, standing and waiting his turn on the bench press. He glanced over at me, and I figured he was thinking, "who let this train wreck in here?" But instead, without hesitation, he rushed over and offered me his towel. Yes, it was sweat-ridden, but the gesture in itself was nice.

Ham wasn't the sharpest tool in the shed. Hell, I don't even think he could spell tool, but he was easy on the eyes and hilarious. His humor was more of the slapstick variety, not the witty sarcasm littered with intelligent references that I had come accustomed to with Lloyd, but it kept me giggling all the same. Mostly, he was a way to occupy my time without obsessing over

Lloyd.

We grew familiar with each other over the course of the semester from the gym and shared a couple mutual friends on campus. Occasionally, he trained me in the gym when he was in between clients. This rainy day in particular though would take our gym sessions to the next level, to the ab machine.

Now maybe I was just vulnerable, but there was something about the fact that a man would sacrifice his towel for me that threw me over the edge. I had clearly been jaded by what I thought was Lloyd's lack of willingness to put me before himself and his job. Looking back, I now saw the unjustness in my comparison, but I was angry and ready to move on.

As I finished my last rep on the ab machine, I reached out to Ham and kissed him. He was caught off guard and looked at me in pure shock. But apparently he had been harboring serious feelings for me - hence, the free training sessions - but had heard from our mutual friends that I was in a long distance relationship. Once it became clear that I was now single and the attraction between us was mutual, within ten minutes, we were doing some serious heavy petting in rain-drenched workout clothes in the backseat of my car.

Our relationship moved pretty quickly. I was caught up in the fantasy of new romance and overcome by the possibility of a real future with someone who lived in my town, who I could see every day and who didn't think twice about blowing off work to catch a movie with me. I'm not sure what his excuse was, but Ham seemed ready to go the distance as well. Within two weeks, he told me he loved me. I replied "me too." Did I mean it? No, but I wanted to.

But after a month, disagreements would turn into shouting matches. It wasn't out of character for Ham to give me a shove or use his body to pin me against a wall while yelling at me. I always chalked it up to being my fault. He never actually hit me or hurt me, and the shouting wasn't one-sided. I could give as well as I took. I was stubborn and never backed down, and I had a horrible attitude. I hate to admit it, but I could also be very belittling.

But infidelity was a deal breaker for me. Ham knew that. We'd often get into it when I thought he was being a little too touchy-feely with his female clients at the gym. It never ceased to amaze me that his older or portlier clients never needed their "core stabilized," as he would put it, but all of his young and perky clientele needed his hands all over their abs. To boot, he was a major flirt and would downplay it as needing to drum up business by word of mouth, insisting that what I thought was flirting was simply him being charismatic in hopes that his clients would refer their friends to him. But again, anyone whose body wasn't already a perfect ten didn't seem to bring out the charisma in him.

The afternoon I caught him with a girl in the hallway of his apartment complex should have been the final straw. He lived in a building near campus so being the sweet little abundance of sunshine that I was, I decided to bring him lunch before my next class. Ok, I wasn't going to class, let's not kid ourselves, but I still had a purchased lunch in tow. But when I got to his floor, I saw him saying goodbye to a perky little thing. His hand was on her ass, and he was telling her how fat it was as I approached the two of them from behind.

Instead of dropping the food and running off like a lady would do, I walked over and smacked him across the mouth. He shoved me into his apartment, and I guess the chick split not wanting to get a smack from me as well. I heard him call down the hall that he'd call her, then he shut his door and came at me screaming that I was interfering with his business. I couldn't believe that he was trying to put this on his personal training. I caught him red-handed in his apartment, not the gym. I got right in his face, yelling as much. He shoved me down, and I jumped right back up to tackle him. After he threw me off of him, he hit me across the face with a closed fist.

What troubled me the most was not that I had been hit by a man, but that I spent the next week hiding my left eye from my son. It melted my heart that I allowed something like this to happen. I had to hide my black and blue eye from him at all costs. My son couldn't understand the depth of what had occurred, but I could and I allowed this to happen to his mother. He loved grabbing my face and nuzzling me, but now I had to deprive him of that simple affection.

I told my parents and others that I got into a fight with a huge lesbian over a parking spot. It may sound rash, but in all reality finding parking spots on campus was no joke. I was too embarrassed and ashamed to tell them the truth. The only one who knew what really went down was Shay, and that's only because she kept pestering me with so many questions in an attempt to track down the mystery lesbian that hit me. I got my story confused and just broke down and told her the truth.

For a while, I was angry at myself. In the past, before I had a child and before Lloyd showed me what real love was, I probably would have stayed in this tumultuous relationship. Lord knows Ham kept trying to apologize and get me back. But now that I was a mother, I couldn't keep relapsing into poor choices. I gave myself a pass for this one instance. I stopped going to the college gym, and Shay would often tag along when I wanted to go audit a class on campus. She knew Ham took those opportunities to try to corner me and beg for forgiveness. She was the best buffer I could ask for. Eventually, he stopped hassling me. I thought he just finally took the hint that we were never ever getting back together, but as I read *Pawns of Love* I learned the real reason.

I was surprised to get a call from Cheyenne. As Ari's best friend, I figured she was calling to ream me about the breakup and not stepping up. I almost didn't answer because I didn't want to hear her reprimands. But she was persistent and on her third attempt to reach me, I picked up the phone.

"Look, Cheyenne, what goes on between me and Ari is none of your business-" I managed to get out before she cut me off.

"He hit her," she shouted.

"What?"

"He hit her. The son of a bitch punched her, and she's sporting a black eye. She won't go to the cops. She's too ashamed, but someone has to do something. He can't get away with this. And the idiot thinks he still has a shot with her and won't stop harassing her," she rattled off.

I got her to slow down and start from the beginning. I couldn't believe what I was hearing. Ari had gotten involved with a guy and he put his hands on her. I was fuming. As soon as we hung up, I went straight to the airport and got on the first flight I could to South Carolina. I didn't even pack a bag. I just grabbed my wallet and left.

A few hours later, I rented a car from the South Carolina airport and crashed at a cheap hotel. It was late, but I couldn't sleep. I stayed up all night watching reruns and infomercials. I had no real plan other than to cause this guy pain. I realized I hadn't stopped clenching my fists since Cheyenne told me what happened. This Graham guy was going to pay.

The next morning, I called Cheyenne. She was astonished that I was in town so quickly. I got the details from her on how to find Graham and headed to the gym first. No luck. He was a personal trainer, but his manager said he didn't have any clients booked for today so probably wouldn't be in until tomorrow. My return ticket had me on a flight back home that night, so I couldn't wait around. I called Cheyenne again, and after some prodding, got his home address.

When I got the complex, I was surprised to see Cheyenne sitting on the steps leading into the building.

"Go home," I told her. "You don't need to be here."

"Dude, your eyes look like you're ready to pillage a small army. I'm just here to make sure you don't do something too rash, something you can't take back that puts you behind bars," she said.

I guessed Ari had told her about an incident before I cleaned up my act where a bar fight had ended with a guy in the hospital and me facing criminal charges. Luckily, security footage cleared me and showed that I was just defending myself, but it was a close call that I never wanted to repeat. But this was Ari. He hit Ari. Rational thinking went out the window.

"Where the fuck he at?" was my only response to her.

I wasn't waiting for her answer. She had already given me the apartment number over the phone. I was too impatient to wait for the elevator so I started up the staircase. Cheyenne was right behind me.

"Ari doesn't know I called you," she said.

"Good. Keep it that way. I won't be sticking around to see her so she doesn't need to know I was here."

"Well, I can't let you go off the rails. I just didn't know what to do when I found out. I thought you'd be more level-headed and convince her to file a report. She'd listen to you. I didn't think you were going to go all caveman - hit first, ask questions later."

"There aren't any questions here. He hit her, and now I'm going to make him bleed."

"Well, I couldn't in good conscience let you kill him and have to spend the rest of your life in jail. That would ruin any chance of you and Ari getting back together," she said sarcastically.

I knew she was trying to defuse the situation a bit and get me thinking more clearly.

"I've got this. You don't have to worry."

"Well then, I should also warn you that Ham's a big

meathead, but he's also about 6'2" and I'd say 250 pounds of pure solid muscle."

"I'm not worried," I said as I finally reached his door. "I know you're in there!" I shouted, pounding on the door. "Open up!"

When the door opened, I stopped myself in the nick of time from landing a jab on a bob-haired brunette who looked scared shitless. The coward had sent a girl to open the door for him. I brushed past her and caught Graham as he was trying to hop out of a window onto the fire escape.

My first punch connected with his jaw and my second hit him square in the eye. An uppercut sent him to the floor. Before I could do any more damage, Cheyenne called out to me. Her words about doing something that could land me in prison and away from Ari for good had taken root.

I grabbed Graham by his collar and looked him in the eye.

"Don't ever even think of looking in Ari's direction again. If I ever hear that you tried to contact her, or that you laid a hand on another female, I will end you."

I kicked him in the gut for good measure just to make sure I'd gotten my point across.

I heard the brunette ask Cheyenne what was this all about. Cheyenne told her that he'd punched her friend.

"He hit a girl. What a douchebag. I'm out of here."

With that, we all exited the apartment.

"I hope your friend's alright," the brunette said to me. "Hopefully this prevents that kind of abuse from happening to someone else. I'm not sticking around to find out though," she said then went on her way.

"You did a good thing," Cheyenne said when we got back to our cars. "Ari's lucky to have you in her life. Why don't you follow me over to her place?"

"I can't. I have to catch a flight back. And, well, I've got some things to work on before I'm ready to see Ari again. Don't tell her I was here, ok?"

"I think you're making the wrong move, but I'll keep this between you and me. She'll never know."

I couldn't believe it. Cheyenne was obviously Shay, and she kept her word and had never told me. I didn't know whether to kick her ass or hug her. But more so, I was overwhelmed by Lloyd's gesture. We weren't even together. Hell, I was sleeping with another man. Yet, he dropped everything, shelled out plane fare and risked his safety and future to fix a problem I had created. Further, he didn't want any recognition for it. He did it solely to make sure I was safe and protected. I kept reading.

The seasons started to change. I started to grow lonely. My buddies decided to take me out one night to get me out of my rut. That's when I met Kim. Kim was a breath of fresh air. Her beauty was undeniable, and she had the wit and intellect to keep up with my verbal sparring. It's not often you get the looks and the personality. At first, she reminded me of Ari and it made me miss her more. But as time went on, Kim made herself stand out and the time I spent with her started to be less about missing Ari and more about enjoying Kim's company for who she was.

I closed the book as a lump grew inside my throat. I didn't want to know about the *other woman*. Nothing could hurt more than learning the details about the one you loved and the woman that replaced you. You can't picture the love of your life having a similar connection with someone that isn't you. Sharing inside jokes, doing little things that you used to do with each other. For years, I tossed and turned imagining them laughing together, making love, and growing old side by side. I played with the idea that he loved her as much as he once loved me, and there were just some questions that you didn't want the answers to. But here they were, in print, right in front of me.

I wasn't ready for the truth. For whatever reason, however, he wanted me to know the truth. It was important enough for him to write a book about it, so I had to continue. But not here. Not out in the open in front of all these New Yorkers and tourists enjoying Central Park.

I hoofed it back home, all the while thinking about the other woman. I wondered if her name was really Kim. Maybe it was a different 'K' name. I remembered seeing her in the bakery, glowing with his child growing inside of her. I wanted to hate her. I wanted to hate him. But there were no bad guys here. Just circumstances. She wasn't a whore or a homewrecker. Lloyd and I weren't together when they met. We were free to date other people, and we were both doing exactly that. Only my dating ended with a black eye led to new life being brought into the world. He'd clearly gotten the better deal, but I'd have to say we both failed at casual hookups.

But who was this woman? Well, she was probably not too different from me. We both found ourselves pregnant out of wedlock. We both fell for Lloyd's good looks, charm and wit. We both wanted a future with him, but only one of us could have it. She'd won there. Still, her love for this man could never possibly match mine, I told myself and clung to that irrational belief. She could never look at him the way I did, but she was still a woman wanting to be loved and to give love in return.

I finally made it back to my place. Reading this would require a glass, or maybe a whole bottle, of wine. I grabbed a glass and took the bottle with me to the couch. I got comfortable and braced myself for what was sure to be a tough read.

CHAPTER EIGHT

The Other Woman

I skimmed through *Pawns of Love*, taking in tidbits of their relationship. Had I been a stranger reading their encounters, I would have thought it was cute, endearing even. My stomach turned as I caught glimpses of another woman holding his attention. Then I came to the part I had been anticipating but also dreading.

The day Kim told me she was pregnant was both the saddest and happiest day of my life. As much as I liked Kim, the thought of closing the book on Ari and Ace forever tore me up inside. I felt sick, but I was also overcome with joy. It was the most bittersweet and odd moment of my life.

I wanted nothing more than to be a father. Then, I pictured Jacob's face. A tear fell from my eye and Kim hugged me in excitement. She had no idea about Ari, Jacob, or the real reason I was crying. My heart ached, but I didn't want this special moment to be overshadowed so I didn't let Kim see the turmoil I was going through. I kept thinking that it should have been Ari giving me this news, and I hated myself for those thoughts. Kim was a great woman. If there hadn't been an Ari, she would have been the perfect woman. I wouldn't mess this up. I wouldn't hurt Kim or my unborn child. I would be the best father and husband if that's what Kim wanted. And that meant forgetting about Ari.

Now, all I had to do was tell Ari. She would inevitably find out, and it was best if she heard it from me. I didn't want to hurt her either although I knew this situation would be just as heartbreaking for her as it was for me. I just didn't know how to do it though. How do you tell the love of your life that any chance of having that life together was over?

For the next few months, I blocked it out of my mind and focused on Kim and planning my child's future. Kim and I were going crib shopping and then I was going to take her to the beach for the weekend. It was something Ari and I had done often when she would visit. I sighed heavily at the thought.

Kim and I were window shopping after looking at cribs, changing tables and other things we'd need for the nursery. Kim and I had gotten a new place together as neither of our former apartments were big enough for a family. And that's what we were now, a family,

We were patiently waiting to cross the street, and I told one of my off-the-wall vulgar jokes. She laughed, but I could tell it was forced. One thing about Ari was that she never had to force it. Neither of us did. It - whatever *it* was - was effortless between us. I remembered a time I had joked with Ari about running away to Oregon.

"Oregon? What's in Oregon? You take me to Oregon and I'll hitchhike outta there faster than a prairie dog during hunting season," she had said.

I smiled at the memory. I immediately pushed the thought aside as it was making my eyes play tricks on me. I could have sworn I saw Ari. I blinked, then my whole world collapsed. With my girlfriend and unborn child by my side, a vision of my past was suddenly before me. But it wasn't a vision. Ari stood ten strides ahead of me, staring at her worst fear.

I felt the breeze pass by my half opened mouth. Before I could even think, Kim was peppering me with questions.

"Who is that? Do you know her? Why do you both look like you've just seen a ghost?"

Ari took off running, and it took everything inside of me not to follow her. I knew I had a lot to explain to Kim, but regardless of my feelings, I was going to be loyal to her and stick by her side through thick and thin. I owed that to her and our child. She had me forever. Even with that being my reality, I had to talk to Ari and explain. I owed her that much, at least.

I explained to Kim that she was my ex. Without going into too much detail, I told her it had been a serious relationship headed toward marriage, but things didn't work out so seeing each other was just awkward. She didn't push me to tell her more, so we just went about the rest of our day and I tried to act as normal as possible.

But that evening, I made up an excuse to get out of the house. I texted Ari: "Meet me at our spot."

I just hoped that she would come. I hoped that I would have the chance to explain and to say goodbye.

Our spot was a place where the sky met the sea, where the world would end and paradise would begin. I, honestly, didn't think she would come. I was sure she had already left to go back home, or wouldn't want to see me. But I would go and I would wait.

I wandered aimlessly down the sandy path that had led me to the love of my life countless times before for happier occasions. This time I would walk down this path toward Ari for the last time. When she appeared in the horizon, she looked like an angel. Her hair was masking her face in the wind, and her sun dress was blown across her body in a way that even a monk's manhood could not ignore. Every feeling I had ever had for this woman came rushing in. I just wanted to touch her, to put my hand against her cheek and embrace her lips with mine. I wanted to take her in my arms and take away all the pain that she was feeling. I could see that she was broken.

I didn't want to face her, so I didn't. I didn't know what to say, so I didn't speak. She asked me if I loved the woman having my child, and my silence told her I did. Then, she said something about not imagining that I could love anyone the way I did her.

But there was an understanding that went without words. I knew that I came second to Jacob in her eyes, and she knew that my child would come before her. I would love my child more than I loved anyone or anything else.

We both looked at each other in pure agony.

Her eyes said, "How could you let this happen?"

Mine responded, "I'm so, so sorry."

The pain was unbearable. Before I knew it, she was walking away from *us*. I wanted so badly to just take off with her, to Oregon, and never look back. Instead, I followed behind her, keeping my distance, all the way to her hotel. I wanted to make sure she was safe. I also wanted to watch her move one last time. My heart sank as she entered her hotel and walked out of my view, this time, for forever.

The fall came and brought with it a promising job opportunity in Los Angeles. My solo endeavor never really took off as Max had taken most of our clientele with him when we parted ways, so I had shopped my resume around town. One of the larger agencies had taken an interest and offered me a position in their LA office. It came with solid pay, benefits and a 401k - things I had to be concerned about with a kid on the way - and Kim was down with the move. Her family was from Seattle, so she was happy to be moving closer to them.

We settled into our new LA home I awaited the December arrival of our daughter. But Ari was never far from my mind. I knew she had started seeing someone. I used a buddy's social media profile to check in on her from time to time. When pictures of her and her new beau cascaded across my friend's computer screen, I felt sick all over again.

It wasn't fair to Kim, but in my mind I kept envisioning Ari being the one that was pregnant. I saw myself holding her hand as she gave birth to our child.

Kim was no fool and after seeing the reaction Ari and I had to seeing one another, she occasionally asked me about it. She had her doubts and concerns, but I became very good at downplaying what Ari and I once had. It was time to focus on my future as a father and husband. I had every intention of proposing to Kim the day she gave birth. I even had the ring hidden in my dresser drawer. But the fucked up part was that I had no clue how to pick out a ring for Kim and subconsciously designed the ring with the jeweler with Ari's hand in mind. In fact, every detail that went into the ring was a detail I knew Ari would appreciate. The ring was designed for Ari, but Kim didn't need to know that.

It was an unusually chilly morning for Los Angeles on December 11 when Kim started having contractions. Being my calm, dapper self, I told her to just breathe in her nose and out her mouth. She threw a pillow at me and told me to go fuck myself. A pleasant seven minute and thirty-five second drive later, we were at Spring Memorial Hospital. The delivery suite was beautiful. Her family had decked it out in pink décor and the baby's outfit to wear home was laid out on what would be my bed for the next two nights.

After seven painstaking hours of labor, and what I thought

would be a severed hand on my part, our beautiful daughter had arrived. Madelyn Grace. She was everything and more than I had ever dreamed and hoped for, bundled up in this delicate little package. Her small hands would clasp over my thumb and I knew there was no greater love than this. It was by far the happiest day of my life. I was a father, and I'd be a damned good one. With all the excitement at hand, I had forgotten all about the ring. I think subconsciously I wanted to forget. I decided to put the ring away and save it for another time.

A week after Madelyn was brought home, I was laying on the hammock in the backyard with the baby on my chest. She stayed calm as she listened to the rhythm of my heart. I was the only one able to calm her since she had been getting colicky. In that moment, I realized the strength a father could give a child by simply assuring them that they were loved and protected.

I examined her pink and white striped onesie, and the pink bow that was tied around her fine black hair, and I sighed in utter happiness. She was the most beautiful girl I had ever seen. She had my nose and her mother's round lips. Her eyelashes were long and thick, and they tickled my cheek as I pulled her closer.

I thought about my father and mentally forgave him for not being built to do what I wouldn't be unable to do. Fatherhood would be my biggest accomplishment in life, and I was ready for every boo-boo, every bedtime story, every anxious feeling, every boyfriend I'd have to threaten with a bat, everything. I thought about my mother and how she had taken on the role of both mother and father. I wondered if she could see Madelyn, if she knew how beautiful she was. I wondered if she was proud of me. I knew all these answers already.

Our first Christmas as a family had been a success. We spent half of the day fussing over Madelyn with family members and taking pictures of her in her red velvet dress. We immersed her in the crumpled wrapping paper and bows left over from the morning. There she modeled for us as we oohed and ahhed over each expression. After the ogling was over, we got her out of that hot dress and into a white onesie. We left in the red and white flowered bow that accented the onesie perfectly. Photo sessions at a halt, we sat down for a dinner that had everything from ham and turkey, to lasagna and veal. Every kind of salad you could imagine, every appetizer, every kind of pie. It was a feast prepared by Kim and her mom.

Dinner was perfect, but I'd be lying if I said I didn't wonder what Ari and her new man were doing at that very moment. I wondered if she made her homemade Oreo cheesecake, which had become a staple at her family's Christmas dinners. I wondered if what's-his-name would enjoy it as much as I did, if he'd appreciate how much work went into it, which I was sure Ari would reiterate over and over again as she had to me each year. Mostly, I just wondered if she was happy, and if she was thinking of me too. I looked over at the clock which read 3:17. I chuckled at the coincidence. March 17 was the day Ari and I met.

My jaw dropped while reading the last passage from Lloyd. I remembered clear as day looking at the clock that same Christmas and it being 3:17. In that moment, I had thought of him and his new family and wondered if he was over me. Goosebumps scattered across my arms as I smiled in delight. You can't make these things up. Fate, destiny, a beautiful design. Not coincidence, not chance. This was bigger than us both. This was beyond anything here on Earth. I continued reading.

As New Year's rolled around, unlike in past years, I had no extravagant plans to don a tux and hit the nightclubs, partying and drinking until four in the morning. Instead, I passed out - from exhaustion, not liquor - around 10 pm, and was awakened about thirty minutes after the New Year had been rung in by the sounds of a screeching child. Kim and I spent the next four hours rocking, swaying, swaddling and trying a number of other soothing techniques to get our colicky princess to settle down.

We were finally able to get some shut eye just before five in the morning. It had been one of the tougher nights we'd experienced so far. But we got through it. Before I headed to bed, as I looked down at my dozing baby girl, I thought to myself, I can do this. I can do the late nights, the early mornings, the constant worrying, the unconditional love no matter the circumstances. I could do whatever it took to soothe and care for my child for the rest of my life. Little did I know how limited that would be.

"Little did I know how limited that would be." I re-read this line over and over in fear of what was to come next. My heart sank at the thought of what this foreshadowed. Was Lloyd ok?

I almost didn't want to read any further, but I had glimpsed an upcoming chapter entitled "The End," and it lured me in. I had to know Lloyd's fate.

> It had been a couple months since I had first noticed my swollen lymph node, but with the excitement of the new baby, I had just sort of swept it under the rug. I had been taking leftover antibiotics that were in the medicine cabinet and I assumed I was just fighting off some infection that would subside on its own. After finally bringing myself to a doctor for some tests, they were a lot more concerned than I imagined. I never expected to hear the words "stage IV lymphoma." I had cancer, and it had spread.

My jaw dropped yet again, but this time in disbelief of what I was reading. Lloyd went on to speak about chemo, about losing his hair, bittersweet moments with his daughter. I could hardly read with the tears flooding down my face. Then a glimmer of hope arose. He finished the book. Surely he survived, somehow someway. He can't be gone. He can't! I made my way to the last page.

> As I anticipated my demise, I held the hand of the woman that had never turned her back on me. As much as she felt she could never live up to my past, she constantly chalked up her own heartache to stick by my side. Kim was the epitome of loyalty. My health was declining, and all I could think about was how empathetic this woman had been. She had so much love for me, and I didn't deserve it.
>
> I knew my daughter and I would be together again one day. I knew that a bond so unconditional would prevail and that a love so powerful would last beyond death. I also had some peace in knowing my daughter was still young enough to be unscathed by all of this. I gave her mother my blessing to find love again and prayed that Kim would bring someone into their life one day who would love my child the way I had and be that father figure she needed.
>
> As I faced my mortality, I reflected on my history with Ari. I yearned for her. I wanted more than anything to see her again, but I couldn't do that to Kim. It was my responsibility to protect Kim's feelings. Until my last breath, I would make her feel as if she was the only one that had my heart. I had to give

her this false reassurance that she was the love of my life when deep down she may have known it was Ari.

The same way I knew my bond with my child would not be broken, I knew my bond with Ari would not either. You don't realize how powerful the soul truly is until you're faced with an end to all ends. I believed now, more than ever, that Ari and I would meet again in the next life. Maybe next time we could get it right. My only wish was for her to know how deeply I always loved her. It would never end.

Pawns of Love fell from my hands and hit the floor with a loud thud. Nodding in disbelief, an overwhelming feeling coursed through my body. This moment should have destroyed me, but it didn't. Instead, a manic feeling overpowered me, and I simultaneously laughed and cried. Lloyd had given me this amazing gift, the gift of truth. I no longer had to toss and turn at night about the what-ifs. I no longer had to beat myself up about the decisions I had made. I was at peace.

I was nonetheless devastated, but an unexplainable weight was now lifted off my shoulders. This man loved me so much that he wrote a book just for me to have answers, just for me to know he never stopped loving me. That, and he always had to have the last word. I remembered argument upon argument where he would text me something random like "peanut" just to have the last word. Here it was in over two hundred pages of text, his last words. I didn't mind so much this time.

Lloyd and I had a mutual understanding through this book. It was that our love stood the test of time and then some. We both knew our love ran deep. Not even death could destroy our bond. I knew in my heart I'd be in his arms again one day. I picked up the book and held it close to my chest. Somehow he had given me the strength I needed to handle this. He always had the ability to give me the courage I lacked, and this was no exception. This book was the message I had been praying for since my mother's passing. It's funny how two great losses can result in such a brave outcome. I was so thankful to Lloyd for saving me once again.

CHAPTER NINE

Reawakening

I realized exactly where I needed to be. Without contemplation I grabbed a duffle bag and started throwing in only my absolute essentials. Toothbrush, panties, leopard print pillow case, and so forth. I topped off my luggage with *Pawns of Love*. After a quick phone call to Gwen to look after my apartment, I was off to hail a cab. Now what would be the odds of getting Lloyd, the Middle Eastern driver again? I looked up to the sky and smiled.

A short drive later and I arrived at JFK International Airport. It was Fourth of July weekend so the airport was packed with travelers. I grew impatient while waiting to purchase a ticket, and my mind found creative ways to keep me entertained. From a young age, I would people watch. As I got older, it turned into a game whenever I was restless. I would look at a stranger from head to toe and try to guess their story.

The man next to purchase his ticket was very tall and burly looking. He had dark hair and a thick brow that was as straight as a space bar. I assumed him to be Russian. His name was Rudolph. He was a contract killer and was here for a hit. The lady behind him was Madame Leary. She had red hair and wore a summer hat reminiscent of, something you would see the gals from *Sex and the City* wearing. She was fancy and was headed somewhere exotic. She most certainly owned a beach house in Florida. As Rudolph approached the counter, I leaned in intently to hear the kill game in his voice. He would surely be angry at having to wait so long, a man of his discrete power. He opened his mouth and this pee-wee Herman voice came out. I burst out laughing and the whole line looked at me. Rudolph, who called himself Max, even looked back. I wasn't worried about it. At this point, I figured I could probably take Rudy.

As I pulled myself together, I thought of how my mother would have loved this story. She was, after all, the one who invented the game for me. She saw early on how observant I was. Instead of just calling me nosy and telling me to mind my own business, she turned my inquisitiveness into a game for me. Countless moments were spent making up vivid and exciting stories for strangers. I often wondered if people did the same for us, and if so who would I be. Morgan the retired porn star? Francesca the Italian spy? Surely they just pegged me as Shelby the bank teller.

Madame Leary was up next. As I leaned in again, I had to jump back. Her strong southern accent caught me off guard. She was loud and a bit vulgar.

"I needa hurry up an' get the hell outta here. My grandkids are waitin', This big ol' apple is too big for me, so let's get on."

Wrong again. It's funny how misleading appearances can be. The old adage "don't judge a book by its cover" was so accurate.

I was finally up to bat and as quickly as possible I got a non-stop ticket to Florida. I had a few hours before my flight, which was good because I had time to hyperventilate. I hated flying.

In all honesty, I wasn't as scared as I usually was. Granted, my limbs were shaking, but I was also really excited. My son had no idea I was coming, and I knew how thrilled he was going to be to see me. We would finally be able to get the closure we both desired.

I stopped at a Dunkin' Donuts shop and got myself a Coolatta. The Coolatta, of course, was to wash down the Xanax. Then, I made my way to my terminal and parked my ass in front of the glass window.

I loved watching the flights come and go, safely. It put my mind at ease but also led me into imaginative daydreams. I thought about the many times I had flown to see Lloyd. The near death experience of flying paired with the anticipation of seeing him was always adrenaline fueled. This time I would be seeing the other love of my life. I missed Renz so much, and this would by far be my most important trip.

♟♚

As I embarked on a montage of memories between my mother, Lloyd, and my son, one in particular stood out. It was the night of my son's birth. It was noon when I started having severe pains that came and went every twelve minutes. My mother called the doctor, and he said to meet him at the hospital. I had been stuffing munchkins from Dunkin' Donuts down my throat when he made the call. She grabbed my bag and ushered me out the door. I went back for one more munchkin.

We arrived at the hospital, and I was five centimeters dilated. The nurse had told me it would happen fast. Ten hours and two epidurals later (the first had come out thanks to a student working on me), still no baby. By this point, I had a fever, and they had to perform an emergency C-section. Throughout the course of the day, I had friends and family in and out. My son's father, however, was at the club. As I received my spinal tap to perform the C-section, they strapped down my hands and gave me a towel to bite. I felt like Hannibal Lector.

Moments later, my son was out. Now I want to say this was the happiest moment of my life, but I'd be lying. I thought it was all the drugs, but I was numb. Time went by, and I was still emotionless. I didn't know it then, but it was post-partum depression. Now, as bad as that got, I was still like a bear with her cub. I was very protective of my son and at times felt heroic. There's an unspeakable knowledge that comes with motherhood. If something happens, your instinct kicks in without even thinking about it. I rescued my son from potential falls, suffocation, mismatched clothes. I was on point.

Although I was physically doing everything I was supposed to, I felt inhuman. But, one day, life made sense again. My son smiled at me. I cried like a wounded dog. Months later, my son grabbed my hand. Months after that, he rested his head on my shoulder. The first time he put his hand on my cheek, I almost died. And when he said I love you, I wanted to melt into the ground. The love that I have for my child is unconditional.

As a parent, you fear heartache for your child. You want to protect them from everything and anything that has ever negatively affected you. You want to spare them that pain that you know so well. Your greatest fear becomes disappointing them. That unconditional love was what drove me to the airport.

My relationship with Lloyd had made me feel human again, made me able to love again. His words, though through his book this time, were once again pushing me forward, pushing me towards the greatest love of all time.

Thinking about the power Lloyd's words had over me brought up another memory. Lloyd had to come to Miami for work, so I drove to South Beach to meet him, leaving Renz with my parents for what I thought would be a quiet, romantic weekend with Lloyd.

I met Lloyd on the beach where he was overseeing a night photo shoot. The plan was for him to be wrapping things up by the time I got there, so we could head out to a late dinner. No matter how many times we saw each other, the excitement never lost its zest. As I approached the beach, I was amused by all the photographers and models. They were promoting a bathing suit line, and the reflection of the moon glistening across the ocean made the perfect backdrop.

Lloyd looked over at me and immediately forgot about anyone else around him. I ran to him, and he picked me up tenderly. He told me he had a surprise for me and took me by the hand to a rack of bikinis. He handed me a turquoise and silver bathing suit and said I was going to be on the cover of the catalogue. My face immediately turned red when I realized one of the models, with her three-inch waist, was also there to, as Lloyd put it, show me the ropes and take me to hair and makeup in a large tent they'd erected on the beach.

I never really lost all the baby weight, and I had so many imperfections.

"Cellulite, stretch marks, gut," was all that I could whisper to Lloyd in response.

He laughed me off and said he could have the photographer airbrush if need be. I didn't want to disappoint him, I didn't want to say no and make him look bad in front of his business partners. Full of doubt and insecurity, I nodded yes.

With the sound of the waves crashing in the background, I was catapulted into hair and makeup. Before I knew it, I was being blinded by flashing lights.

"Just relax," the photographer said impatiently.

How could I relax when all I could think about was the junior bacon cheeseburger I ate on the drive down? For sure it was showing. I was just lucky it was only a junior and not a double. I kept trying to suck in, but I could feel my ass jiggling. I looked over at Lloyd in a panicked frenzy. Some model was chatting him up and giggling. I didn't think he had noticed the distress I was in. Until, of course, a song started playing from one of the laptops. And it wasn't just any song, it was my song. It was a song that I had often used to make videos for Lloyd to get him through those long separations from me. It was my feeling sexy song.

I saw Lloyd standing at the laptop. "You're going to do fine. You're beautiful, baby," he said.

Once I heard that, it was a wrap. I felt so confident, so beautiful. The whole crew was oohing and ahhing and talking about how amazing I was. I knew Lloyd was proud of me.

When the catalogue came out, I was surprised to find Lloyd at my doorstep. Flowers, fruit arrangements, clothes - those were the norms, but to see Lloyd in the flesh was a surprise, a welcomed one but a surprise no less. He was holding flowers and the catalogue.

I had just gotten off from work and hadn't picked up Renz from my parents' house yet. I got out of the car and quipped, "Are you with the Publishers Clearing House?"

"Yeah, I sure am and today's your lucky day," Lloyd played along.

"Well, what did I win?"

"You won all of this, baby," he said, exaggeratedly while doing a dance.

Then, he bear-hugged me and handed me the catalogue. I was pissed.

"Nothing has been edited!" I shouted. "No photoshopping or anything. It's just all me, completely uncensored with cellulite and all."

"Calm down," Lloyd said. "It's perfect. Now go pack an overnight bag. I already made arrangements for Renz to stay with your parents."

I was heated, but I still did as requested although I sulked for most of the car ride. We ended up in Tampa with a suite at the Hard Rock Casino for the night as Lloyd tried to make amends for his broken promise.

As the evening progressed, my mood didn't. Lloyd got us a couples' massage and tried to reach over and rub my head. I slapped his hand away. He took me for a lobster dinner. I told him it sucked, even though it was exquisite.

Granted, I was being childish, but I was so angry at him. This was my unconcealed, flawed body for the world to see. I was mortified, and he had promised. As we got drinks and hit the slots, I could see Lloyd was getting fed up with my attitude. He reached in for a kiss and I held my glass up in front of my mouth.

"Ok, Leann, stop being a spoiled brat. Look, I'm sorry that I didn't photoshop it, but the truth is you don't need to be photoshopped. Did you know this catalogue has brought in double the inquiries of the spring edition?"

I looked at him in disbelief. But honesty was Lloyd's only policy.

"You're the most beautiful girl I have ever seen. You need to learn to love yourself. In order to give and receive love, you gotta love yourself first," he said, looking me dead in the eye with sincerity.

Those were some of the realest words ever spoken to me. That sentence alone helped me fight my demons and boosted my self-esteem. It even helped me be a better mother. After all, how could I teach someone to be a confident, self-assured person if I didn't have confidence in myself.

As Lloyd went on about how he couldn't censor me because to him I was flawless, and even my imperfections were perfect, I cut him off, pulling him into a deep kiss. Of course afterwards, I asked him to tell me again how no other girl could touch me.

I thought we'd be leaving in the morning so Lloyd could get back to work, but he told me we had the day off. We had the suite for one more night if we wanted it, or he said we could also go back to my place and spend time with Renz if I preferred. I loved that he was so thoughtful when it came to my son, but Renz was scheduled to spend the weekend with his father so I was free to give Lloyd my undivided attention.

Together, we were like two big kids. We spent the afternoon doing handstands in the pool and playing hide and seek throughout the casino. We took advantage of being work- and child-free for a full 24 hours and made love at least five times in the daytime alone - on the dresser, in the shower, the parking garage, even in a conference room downstairs.

We decided to do a low-key early dinner and just order room service. We fed each other like newlyweds. As it got dark, we got ready to hit the club scene, adhering to our ritual of getting dressed while playing our favorite songs. Lloyd and I would sing to each other. Our favorite duo to duplicate was Ja Rule and Ashanti. Of course, I mastered the part of Ja while Lloyd belted out Ashanti's lyrics.

We decided to hit the downstairs club where we danced all over each other like dogs in heat. Then, we hit the casino. I sat on his lap at the roulette table, and he made me kiss his chips for luck. I felt like the characters from *Indecent Proposal*, minus Lloyd giving me to another man for the night for money. We didn't win big, but we were winning already.

♟

As a flight let out at my terminal, I wondered how many people getting off board were going to be reunited with their children. I saw an Asian family get off the flight, and all five family members - a mother, father, boy and two girls - held hands. I thought it was adorable. Kind of weird, but adorable nonetheless. The boy looked over at me and motioned to "web" me like Spiderman.

A half hour later, my flight began to board. Cabin after cabin was called. I was in C so when they called me, I had already been in line posing as a B. I was first to get on in my section and by far the most terrified. As I took my seat, I checked my seatbelt no less than seventeen times, as if a seatbelt would help me when the plane plummeted to my fiery death. I started talking to myself but only in my head, not out loud. First it was counting, then nursery rhymes, then attempting to list all the presidents. I had a good four off hand.

Before I knew it, we were taxiing down the runway and the flight attendants were showing us how to use the floating devices. I always made it a point to play close attention.

As the flight took off, I started with my usual "Oh God, oh God, oh God" I know, I probably sounded like I was orgasming. My attempt to hide my prominent fear of flying was an epic fail. The flight attendant immediately tried to calm me down, I'm sure it was her way of trying to shut me the hell up, so I didn't frighten the others.

I couldn't help it. The scene from *Final Destination* would repetitively play in my head whenever I got on a plane by myself. It was a battle that only my mother and Lloyd ever understood. Here I was, left all alone, to fight the thoughts that consumed me and paralyzed me with fear. As soon as drinks were being served, I got a glass of tequila. Not a shot, a cup. Not even fifteen minutes later, the plane endured great turbulence. I was screaming in horror. I think the flight attendants wanted to punch me.

Out of nowhere a calming feeling came over me. I could

almost feel my mother holding my hand. I looked at the vacant seat next to me and started smiling.

"Hi, Mom," I whispered as to not look schizophrenic.

With my luck, the first flight attendant that tried to console me was looking straight at me with her brows turned inward.

I looked up at her and said, "What the hell did you give me? Moonshine?"

She didn't laugh. Lloyd would have laughed. I turned and smiled, looking out the window as the turbulence subsided.

It was smooth sailing from then on out. My plane landed in beautiful Florida an hour and a half later. The very first thought that entered my mind was Publix subs. I missed those damn sandwiches. Then, I thought about my father and brother. I was never particularly close with them, but I knew they'd be happy to see me. I felt like I had become a physical reminder of my mother to them, and that knocked down some of the walls between us. I was excited to see my nephews, whom I always called and checked in on. I was also excited to tell Renz that grandma was still around, that I'd felt her presence when I was on the plane, and that he could rest assured that she was watching over him as well.

One escalator ride later and I was outside. Prior to reading Lloyd's book, the smells and feel of Florida probably would have upset me as there were so many reminders of my mother. But now I knew what I had known all along. The experience on the plane was definitely not the result of alcohol. It was real. Now Lloyd would have called me a nut job, but I knew Renz would believe me. He shared my same quirky spirit, and he could sense things too. Reading the end of Lloyd's book gave me a sense that he had finally understood the power of love and accepted that it had no expiration.

I rented a car and made my way to Marc's house. On the drive over, I thought about whether I should tell Renz about Lloyd. Our breakup had hit him pretty hard. I didn't know if it was worth opening old wounds. But Renz adored Lloyd, so I also didn't know if it was fair to keep something like this from him. I ultimately decided that the loss of his grandmother was more than enough for such a young boy to handle. He didn't need to be burdened with this as well. My hour drive came to a halt as I approached Marc's street.

Renz was outside playing ball with his cousins. The car's windows were tinted, and I was wearing sunglasses, so he had no idea I was in the car. I saw him motion me to hurry up, so they could continue their street ball. I laughed so hard and then pulled up. As I put the car in park, I admired my little grown boy. He was perfect. He had overcome so much heartache. A child is supposed to relish dreams, fantasies, and imagination. They should envision forever as an attainable concept and should not have to have that vision stomped on by the harsh truth of reality.

My son was an exception. I believe he was put on this specific journey because he was strong enough to handle it. I got out of the car, took off my glasses and waited for him to look over.

"Ma?!"

I smiled and tears came down my face as he ran over and hugged me. "I missed you, baby."

"I missed you too, Mom."

I told Renz that we were going to go see his grandmother the next morning. He was so happy but also apprehensive. He wanted to visit her grave but couldn't do it alone, and he knew how hard it was for me.

That night, Renz and I were going to sleep at my brother's house. He lived right near the cemetery. First, I wanted to go visit my dad. Renz had already seen his pop, because Mark was pretty good about that kind of stuff. I asked Renz how he was doing, and Renz said he was good, but going gray. As we approached my parents' home, I got a lump in my throat. I wished somehow I'd open the door and see my mother, but I knew I wouldn't. Renz was anxious to get out of the car, but I grabbed his arm and told him I had to tell him something.

I told him how much I loved him and he said he knew and that he loved me too. As we entered their home, my father greeted us with open arms. I couldn't help but cry when he embraced me. I loved my father, and I hated that we weren't closer. There was a lot of regret, yet a lot of stubbornness paired with it. I often dwelled on what was lost and didn't want to focus on what could be regained. I made a conscious decision to build a relationship with him now. Hugging my dad gave me a sense of security. I needed a parent's love in this moment more than ever.

I wished I could tell my dad about Lloyd, but he didn't even know anything about him. Maybe one day I could write it all out the way my mother often had. I was much better with written word. I wanted someone to coddle and comfort me for the loss I was grieving privately. I no longer had Lloyd's big arms for consoling. As my father and I broke away, I noticed him wiping away tears discretely. It was the typical man cry where the tears don't necessarily flow but they just build up in the corner. Then, the man pretends he has something in his eye and just sort of pokes himself.

It was endearing. Renz, my father, and I spent hours laughing and reminiscing about mom. We played home videos and my dad made us burgers. I could tell he was lonely. He was so excited to have company and just have someone to talk to. My father adored my son, and I started second-guessing my decision to move Renz away from him, and away from Marc too for that matter. Renz's cousins were here, his aunts and uncles. I decided if Renz wanted to move back, we would. But I didn't bring it up. I thought it best that we talk about it when we got back to New York.

It was time to head to my brothers, and I invited my father to come with us. It was as if his bag was pre-packed because five minutes later we were on the road. On the car ride over, it was as if Renz had read my mind.

"Mom, I miss living here," he said.

Truth be told, although I loved the vibe of New York, I was starting to realize that my *Sex and the City* fantasies were being played out as the spend all your money on a closet-sized apartment and freeze your ass off for seven months out of the year rendition. I had enough money put away that I could sublet the apartment until my lease was up and afford a down payment on a house in Florida.

Before I could open my mouth, my father chimed in, "You guys could live with me."

It was a bit impractical and downright scary to think about moving back in with my dad at my age, but there was a house for sale on his block. I would look into it and told them as much. After a forty-five-minute discussion, the ball was in motion. We had a game plan, and all parties were content. I felt I was finally getting the closure I needed to overcome all the pain and move past it without running from it.

As we got out of the car to enter my brother's house, Renz ran ahead and I stopped my father. I looked at him as seriously as possible. It was the hardest thing for me to say, but I told my father he didn't have to be alone if he didn't want to. I would be ok with him moving forward. I felt like he deserved love and happiness again. He smiled and said he wouldn't be alone anymore because we were moving back. I smiled back and hugged him compassionately.

My brother and his wife welcomed us with open arms. My sister-in-law and I popped open a bottle of wine and traded stories about our kids. We had all boys, so the theme of discussion was the crazy things that boys do. Later that night, she and I went upstairs, and she told me that she was pregnant. It was a complete surprise to my brother and her and they were hoping for a girl. My mother's birthday was nearing, so they thought to tell my dad on that day to take away some of the grief. We joked about how maybe it'd be the reincarnation of my mother, and the child would be an avid cleaner.

"I'll get him or her a stuffed vacuum," I quipped.

I went back downstairs and saw all the men glued to an Xbox. As I stood on the stairwell peering over them, I felt so complete. I knew my mom was seeing the very vision that I was and I knew she was smiling alongside me. Renz looked over at me and smiled. I had overheard him telling his cousins he was moving back. Had I not come on this trip, none of this would be happening. It was surely fated.

I went into the guest room where I would be sleeping and called Shay. I was going to meet up with her the following night. She pressed me about the book, but I told her I'd tell her in person. I felt that speaking of Lloyd's death would make it that much more real. Jax and Shay had stopped speaking when Lloyd and I had. Shay, a Scorpio like me, was very stubborn. I knew she had deleted him out of her phone along with any social media they had kept contact on. I was sure she had no idea about his death. I understood why she kept the incident with Graham concealed from me, but she would have told me something like this.

That night, I could not get comfortable. Tossing and turning, I wondered what Lloyd's last days had been like. He always told me he didn't fear death; he feared an empty life. I could sense his courage throughout the book, and I was positive he wasn't fearful. I knew his main concern was getting that message to me, so that when I did learn of his death, I would know how he truly felt up until the end. You couldn't make this stuff up. Our love was transcendent even through the most painstaking obstacles.

I ended up crying myself to sleep. I wasn't sad. I was just overcome with emotion. What people don't think about after a loss is how lucky they were to have had that person in their life, even if it were for a brief time. We become so focused on the loss itself that we don't appreciate what we gained from knowing that individual. That person that we were blessed with in our lives, others would never get to know. We were granted that time, and for that I was thankful.

CHAPTER TEN

Closure

The next morning, I awoke to the smell of bacon and eggs. I hadn't woken up to that smell since my mother had been alive. Although I cooked, and cooked well might I add, Renz was a picky eater so we went out a lot. Breakfast in New York consisted of a bagel and croissant sandwich from our corner deli. We frequented the deli every weekend, and the deli owner had our sandwiches ready before we even stepped in.

I walked downstairs to find the boys inhaling food as if it were their last meal. I looked at Renz in shock – you would think I never fed the kid. Nonetheless, I was pleased to see him enjoying a meal. I wandered over to the assembly line where everyone appeared to be on their second round, and I fixed myself a plate.

"How did you sleep?" my sister-in-law asked.

"Great," I said.

I overheard my son making plans for when we moved back and I smiled to myself. I felt as though this whole trip was orchestrated by my mother and Lloyd. I felt as though I could still count on them.

After breakfast, I packed an overnight bag for my reunion with Shay. We were going to meet up with a few other friends that night, and I'd just crash at her house so not to disturb the family if it ended up being a late night. Renz and my father were going to hang out at my brother's house for another night. I was counting on Shay to help me figure out what to tell Renz about Lloyd.

I couldn't lie to my son, but I thought it best to withhold certain information. He was on such a high note about moving back, and I didn't want him to know about Lloyd's passing just yet. Just as I was finishing up getting my bag ready, Shay called.

"Where you at, be-otch?" she said endearingly.

I could always count on Shay to brighten my mood. We made plans to meet for sushi, where we would catch up, and then we would head out to our favorite bar. We spent so much time at the place, every bartender there knew our names.

Before I headed to the Ville - the Ville being Springville, where I had grown up, - there was just one thing left to do. Renz walked in the guest room and looked at me with a knowing look. I knew it was time.

The whole family got into two cars and headed to Gabbyshore Memorial, where mom was laid to rest. Although we all decided to go together, everyone agreed that Renz and I would get a few moments to ourselves with mom before the others joined since it would be our first visit.

As we wound around the bumpy road to the far end of the cemetery, a lump grew in my throat. Even though I believed so adamantly that she was still around, there was something so unreal about it all.

My father put that car in park and looked over at me, but said nothing. We both knew how difficult this was. We didn't need clichéd condolences. In fact, I didn't want anyone to speak. I just wanted to process this on my own. He did, however, put his hand on my shoulder and gave me a squeeze. I closed my eyes for a moment and then peered over at the gravesite that he pointed out. I looked in the rearview mirror to see Renz already in tears, and I clenched my lips in an attempt to be strong for him.

After a deep sigh, I said, "Let's do this, baby."

We both were hesitant, but we managed to get out of the car and shut the doors behind us. My brave, brave son reached over and took my hand.

"It's ok, Mom."

Renz and I made our way to what I once would have considered just a heap of grass. The whole idea of a gravesite used to infuriate me, but now I had a little more peace with it.

As we got closer, it was absolutely beautiful. With so many flowers, it was clear that so many people must have been visiting her and frequently. The area was so well kept although, for my tastes, the tombstone could have had a little zebra or leopard print to really make it pop. I started redecorating it in my mind. This would be my new obsession. I'd maintain my mother's gravesite and make sure it was the nicest in the whole cemetery. I realized my coping strategy of ignoring the true situation was kicking in and I tried to snap out of it and let the realness sink in. Just then, a breeze blew one of the arrangements aside, revealing the words mother and grandmother on the tombstone. I dropped to my knees and lost it.

I felt everyone's eyes on me. I didn't want to look up, but I could feel my son staring at me. I had to pull it together. Renz knelt down beside me and put his arm around me.

"Don't worry, Mom. We'll see her again."

I suddenly stopped crying, pulled my hands away from my face and looked at him in amazement. Such a young man, yet so smart. I knew that he meant what he said. I knew he believed that as much as I did.

"I know, baby, I know."

How quickly the roles had changed. I wrapped my arms around him as we sat in silence, admiring, remembering, and appreciating.

It felt like an eternity went by before the rest of the family joined us. Renz and I got up and dusted ourselves off as we all stood in awe. We all embraced each other, hugging, crying, and laughing. This was such a bittersweet moment that I felt gave us all peace. That day would be a turning point for us all. Relationships and familial bonds would strengthen from that point on.

We all piled into the vehicles and headed back to my brother's house. I was ready for a drink. Even though it was only 3 pm, I knew it was five o'clock somewhere. I kissed Renz goodbye and thanked everyone for such an incredible day. I then got in my Pontiac G6 and headed north, to the Ville. I hadn't been away for that long but in our town even moving away for a month was a major accomplishment. Things didn't change much in our town. The same people frequented the same spots and stayed in the same crowds. I was still looking forward to seeing what hadn't changed.

♟♟

Forty minutes later, I was at Wasabi, a local sushi bar. The restaurant was dim, but I immediately spotted the back of Shay's head when I heard her whining about having too much ice. It was typical Shay, complaining and loud-mouthed. Saying hi and having that dramatic long hug would be too generic. I decided scaring the shit out of her was a better move. I crept behind her, and as predicted, she jumped up and screamed. She threatened to kick my ass while hugging me tightly.

I looked at her, acknowledged her now red hair, and smiled profusely. I had missed her desperately. Not many people could understand my passion in the way that Shay could. I knew when I told her the story she would laugh with me, cry with me, hyperventilate with me, and so forth. She always understood the love I had for Lloyd and vice versa. I was quiet at first because I knew the vibe was about to be destroyed. I listened as she told me about her guy drama, I shook my head in disgust when needed. I gave her advice when I could get a word in. Then, I was up.

I waited for our second round of warm sake to be delivered, then I began. As my mouth went a mile a minute, I saw the excitement in Shay's expression. She hung on my every word, and she showed as much astonishment to the revelations in the book as I had. As her jaw dropped lower and lower, I kept saying "I know, crazy, right?" She tried to apologize for not spilling the beans Lloyd's run-in with Graham, but I told her there was no need. They were both just trying to protect me. I took a shot of sake and then laid the last chapter on her.

Her face changed from hot to cold in a matter of seconds. Her face was pale white, and she clasped her hands around her mouth and started to cry. I felt like everything was happening in slow motion, and my face started breaking as I uttered the words, "He's gone."

I found myself consoling Shay rather than her consoling me. She couldn't understand. Then, she apologized and asked me how I was keeping it together so well. Her explanation was that I was in shock, but I explained it was something so much deeper than anyone could understand. I was ok because I was in on a secret that millions would never have the opportunity to discover - pure, whole-hearted, unadulterated, true love. Soul mates, a concept thought to only exist in movies, were real. It was a love that would last for an eternity, no matter which plane of existence we were inhabiting.

She nodded in agreement, but I knew she was just trying to give me solace and appease me. Whatever it was that kept me together, she wanted to humor it. I knew not even Shay could completely understand what Lloyd and I had. The waitress made her fifteenth stop at our table and before even asking, we both shouted, "Another round."

We laughed at our synchronized response. After we finished up and waited for the check, I decided to give Shay some positive news and told her we were moving back. Shay was Renz's godmother, so naturally she was excited, but she couldn't help but make a smart ass comment. "Aw, poor Gwen. Hope she had fun borrowing you."

At this point we were both a little intoxicated, so we called a friend to pick us up. Moments later, it was Eric Vendel to the rescue. Eric was an old friend to the both of us. Shay and I had both casually dated him throughout our middle and high school careers, but no bad blood accumulated. We all stayed close friends over the years and had formed a sibling type of relationship. Maybe it was a bit of a Kansas sibling, but we were all close nonetheless. His silver Camry etched towards us, and Shay jokingly stuck out her thumb.

"How much?" Eric demanded.

"For you, we'll call it a freebie," I said with the intoxication highlighting my tone.

We threw ourselves into his car, and it felt like high school all over again. Shay and I hadn't been this drunk together since prom. I thought back to how little had changed. On prom night, Shay and I would rush off to the bathroom where we shared a flask of Malibu Rum. Eric was with our arch nemesis Brandy Meyers, and Shay and I plotted on ways to make her trip. I was either going to step on the train of her dress or Shay would spill a drink in her path. Neither plan ended up playing out. We had gotten so drunk that we ended up passing out in our limo with our dates frustrated and sexless.

We did wake up by the time the limo pulled up to the beach strip our hotel was on. Again we left our dates hanging as the two of us thrill seekers ventured out. We hopped from hotel party to hotel party, and I remembered, at one point, smoking marijuana in an empty tub with Shay and a couple of friends from our math class. That would be the last time I'd ever smoke because it made me see a lizard on my friend Pete's shoulder. It was not just any lizard. This lizard whistled at me at one point to find out if he had a shot.

He didn't but my high school sweetheart Bret, who'd broken up with me two months before prom, did. We found ourselves hooking up in the stairwell of the hotel he was staying in. His poor girlfriend and my poor date would never know, and neither of us would ever forget.

Prom coincided with college kids' spring break so the Clearwater strip was bombarded with prom-goers and spring breakers. The nicest hotel on the strip, which Bret was staying at, was also holding a bar mitzvah. As Bret and I rekindled our flame, a Jewish boy walked in on us and scurried down the stairs apologizing as he passed. Bret and I could not stop laughing as all we caught was a glimpse of his yarmulke. It was a memory permanently etched into my mental yearbook. For years to come, we would bring it up whenever we ran into each other.

By the end of prom night, Shay and I didn't know how to explain our antics to our dates, so we pretended to pass out on the couch that sat in our mutual suite. We giggled silently and peeked at each other each time they'd try to wake us. She was my partner in crime, and our free spirits were untamable.

♟♟

Sitting in the back of Eric's car, I could see the way Shay and him were looking at each other. Their flame was still very much alive, and I smiled at the endless possibilities for love. I looked out the window and wondered what my own future would bring. I amused myself with the idea that Lloyd was somewhere guiding my every move and deciding my future husband for me. I gave him so much credit for the woman I grew into. He always pushed and challenged me and never gave up on me. I knew he would be proud of the current decisions I was making.

It took me a long time to realize I didn't have to be this insane idea of perfection for Lloyd to love me. He broke down my walls and insecurities and showed me that even my imperfections were beautiful to him, and that was what enabled me to prosper. I knew and accepted, because of him, that failures were not measured by failed attempts, but by not attempting at all. I strived every day for more. I decided in that short car ride to the bar that I would set out to open my own publishing company when I returned to Florida. It was something I went back and forth with for many years but didn't have the courage to do. Now I had that courage.

As we approached Kokomo's, I saw a familiar car. It was Bret's Lexus. I grinned at the thought of hearing the story of the Jewish boy for the umpteenth time. It was funny how much stayed the same in the Ville. I walked into the bar and the same doorman,

Sal Mourmando, who doubled as a bar back and DJ when needed and had been there since I was twenty-one, greeted me with a hug and asked me about New York. He was from Brooklyn and had offered encouraging words that helped influence my decision to actually go for it and leave.

I remembered those words so vividly. "Free yourself from heartache and write not just a new chapter to your life, but a new book altogether," he said.

That stuck with me. Who's to say life is one book and not several volumes? I told Sal about my impromptu decision to move, and he thought it was a great idea. In that moment, his approval felt almost as good as Lloyd's would have.

That memory was cut short as I was being bombarded with lemon drop shots. Shortly after, Bret came over and picked me up.

"Hey, Moonie," he said, using a nickname I picked up in middle school over an unfortunate moon pie incident. I couldn't complain too much about the name though as Bret's nickname was Mooby because he had man boobs when we were younger. No one let him forget it even though his body took a turn for perfectly chiseled freshman year of high school.

Bret was looking really, really good partly because he was my high school sweetheart and partly because I just had three back-to-back lemon drops. The temptation to crash another bar mitzvah wasn't far from my mind. While people around me were laughing and cheering, a red flower caught my eye. A young girl probably in her early twenties was rocking a side swept bun with a red carnation sticking out.

This young girl's hair reminded me of a conversation that Lloyd and I once had as we imagined our wedding. I was one of those girls who had been planning my wedding since I was ten years old. The affair had evolved as I matured, and the latest rendition was developed when I was nineteen. I even had a little scrapbook with images of dresses that I wanted to splice together. One dress had the right top, the other the right train, and so on. My hair would be in a side swept bun with a red flower, and my lips would be painted red. Red rose petals would be embedded throughout my train. My hard-on for Bret was slowly dwindling.

♟

Lloyd and I were together, staying in a New York hotel for the weekend that his company was scoping out for future events. It was funny how neither of us would ever talk about relocating, yet our future plans always included each other. We'd talk about the interior design of our future home. We'd talk about our future kids' names. We would even talk about a honeymoon in Bali or Nepal, riding elephants in the water and making love until our bodies gave out.

It was a white winter in New York when I had flown in on a whim. Lloyd was at the airport to greet me, and since my flight had a long, unplanned layover in Tennessee, I was starving. He suggested we go to one of his favorite Indian places in Soho and my stomach turned immediately. I wasn't sure that my stomach could handle all the strong flavors and spices Indian food was known for, but as usual Lloyd convinced me it would be an experience worth trying.

As we were ushered to a tight corner in the closet-sized restaurant, I began to sweat. Lloyd noticed and comforted me with, "Just wait 'til you taste the paan."

What appeared to be an Indian rendition of salsa made its way into the deep layers of my tongue, and without second guessing myself, I practically poured my glass of water down my face. Lloyd couldn't stop laughing and I wanted to throw his beloved paan in his face.

As soon as our waiter made eye contact, I shouted "alcohol!" The waiter informed us that we'd have to go to the Indian liquor store downstairs. We had to go underground to get imported Indian booze? What the hell? Lloyd assured me it was protocol, but I was sure that the imported Indian beer would no doubt act as absinth and have me seeing fairies.

Lloyd escorted me downstairs where we bought some beer to take back to the table. While paying for the alcohol, I noticed an array of postcards near the cash register and one card in particular stuck out like a sore thumb. It was Miami Beach, but what stood out was the color scheme of the sunset.

"Lloyd, baby, that's my dream."

I had told Lloyd on numerous occasions of a recurring dream I had been having since I was ten years old. It was my idea of what heaven looked like. The color patterns were unimaginable, and here the same exact image that had been confined to my subconscious for so long stared me in the face.

Poor Lloyd probably never believed half of the shit I came up with. At least that's what I had thought before reading his book. He still humored me regardless.

"Maybe that's where we're meant to get married," he

responded matter-of-factly.

For once, I was speechless. I couldn't believe what he had just said, and he'd said it so nonchalantly as though it wasn't a big deal.

When we got back to the table, he scarfed his curried lamb, sweat dripping down his face from the spices, and I guzzled my beer in anticipation. At this point, I just hoped he'd find me more attractive than his dinner. He finally looked over and asked me if I was going to eat. Looking at my plate, we both noticed I had only taken three bites. It was actually rather good, but I was eager to hear more about this wedding.

"So will we be in casual wear for this beach wedding? Are you planning on wearing thong sandals? Am I in a flowery sundress? Tell me."

Lloyd looked a bit frightened as he always did when beer and passion took me over. He laughed at my seriousness and said, "Me and my groomsmen are wearing black and red while your bridesmaids are in short red dresses. You've got a red flower in your hair and sexy red lips."

I gasped and my eyes widened. How could his plans match mine so well? There was no way he had army crawled his way through my mother's attic and found my wedding planner. He wasn't as meticulous as I was when it came to that detective crap, nor was he short enough to finagle around up there.

"That's, at least, what Shay told me would be happening at our wedding," he said, bursting out laughing.

"You jerk," I responded and threw a piece of bread at him.

"You should have seen the look on your face," he said, still laughing. "As long as you're there, I don't really care what I have to wear. But I do want a marble cake. You know, to show everyone how a mix of chocolate and vanilla goes so well together," he joked.

As Lloyd struggled to keep his nose from running from all the spicy food he was continuing to scarf down, I looked at him with pure admiration. He was the man of my dreams and there was no doubt in my mind we would be married one day. Even though neither of us could make that leap and relocate, we still couldn't picture our lives without each other. We would continue to fight for a future together.

After we finished up at the Indian restaurant, we made our way back to the hotel. I was freezing my Floridian butt off, so we decided to sit in the lobby which had a fireplace and a machine for hot chocolate. I could never explain to anyone how safe Lloyd made me feel. No matter where we were, what we were doing, where I was meeting him, I felt entrenched with protection. He made me feel invincible, like we could face anything together. I could conquer my biggest fears with Lloyd present in my mind.

We sat on the suede couches, hot cocoa in hand, and watched reruns of Friends on the lobby television. It was getting late, but we were in the city that never sleeps, so the constant flow of hotel guests didn't let up and I was starting to catch a chill from the cold air let in each time the hotel doors opened.

Lloyd had been rubbing my shoulders for a good ten minutes before I felt the tension building up. The heat was present, and it wasn't left over from the meal, nor was it penetrating from the fire. It was our bodies calling out for each other. He grabbed my shoulders tighter and tighter and then wrapped his right hand firmly around my neck. I let out a discrete moan, and he pulled my head back by my hair. I turned around and made sure the coast was clear, then without a care in the world, I slipped my hand down Lloyd's pants. My appetite at dinner was suppressed as I was apparently saving it for dessert. I retrieved my hand and made a beeline for the elevator.

As soon as the elevator doors closed, Lloyd slipped his fingers inside of me. Elevators and stairwells were my craft by this point. Each floor we'd pass, the excitement of getting caught would grow. We made it to our floor unseen, but the game wasn't over. I pushed him into a shallow hallway that held the washer and dryer for that floor, and there we let any inhibitions were holding onto in the lobby and elevator go. He ripped my pants off, which I would later complain about, but in that moment didn't mind. He lifted me up onto the dryer, teasing me at first but then giving me the full depth of his member.

After we had both been satiated, he put his coat on me and piggy backed me to the room, so my ripped pants would go unnoticed. As we made our way to our door, we noticed a couple that may or may not have played witness to our escapade. All we could do was apologize and then burst out laughing once the electronic key card let us into our room. That night we ordered room service and laughed until our stomachs hurt about the laundry room rendezvous.

♟♟

With a large grin on my face, Bret asked me what I was

thinking about. Not wanting to hit him with my dead ex, I said I was thinking about prom night. Bret started telling the story to everyone that would listen, and I ordered another drink. Shay, who could practically read my thoughts, put her hand on mine and asked if I was ok. I really was. I was blessed to even be able to have these memories, and they were what would keep me going, keep me believing.

Two rounds later, our friend Jack suggested we all go to a nearby karaoke bar. It was kind of tradition when my group of friends would get together - get drunk and sing. Luckily, the bar was only a block away, so we walked over. Bret lit up a cigarette, and I took a drag in my drunken stupor. I had this thing about thinking I was the sexiest woman alive when I was inebriated. Lloyd called it my stripper ego. I took another puff of his cigarette and blew it out seductively. Although I wasn't ready to move on, there was no harm in flirting.

We made our way to the karaoke bar, and I was first up. I chose to sing "Because You Loved Me" by Celine Dion. It was a song that I had once dedicated to my mother. I belted the lyrics out as if I was competing on the season finale of American Idol. While singing the lyrics "I'm everything I am because you loved me," I just broke down. I didn't want to be the emotional drunk, but the song was so powerful and brought up feelings about both my mother and Lloyd.

My friends were quick to my rescue. The girls helped me off stage as the guys prepared to do their rendition of the Backstreet Boys' greatest hits. My girlfriends and I broke out the singles and started showering them with money. We were cheering them on and I attempted to whistle by putting my pinky's in the corners of my mouth, but I had never whistled a day in my life. I ended up just blowing air tinged with spit. After they finished up "I Want It That Way," the girls were up. We decided to take it back old school.

Although there were five of us, we decided on "Baby Love" by The Supremes. Cutting each other off and trying to steal each other's shine was not uncharted territory for us. Like a bunch of drunk sailors, we tried our very best to keep it classy. My friend Brittany may have flashed her boobs at one point, but then we were unstoppable. We even threw in some choreography. I winked at Bret and gestured as though I was throwing my panties at him. It was gold. An hour later, we were kicked out for being belligerent.

Arm-and-arm, Bret and I made our way to the curb. Everyone else was hanging out in the parking lot between the bars as well. We spent much of high school hanging out in parking lots before we were of age to get into the clubs and bars. I longed for the days of our innocence. Well, we weren't exactly innocent, but we did use a few more brain cells before getting wasted, such as engaging in intricate scavenger hunts and playing manhunt.

Bret chuckled as he pointed over to the McDonald's where we lost our virginity to each other. Yes, extremely romantic, it was after hours in the McDonald's parking lot where my flower was soiled. This was before our McDonald's was open twenty-four hours, and thankfully before social media had become so big. Our group had been sipping on a few cases of Smirnoff Ice, and Bret and I found ourselves having a hard time figuring out how a condom worked. I remembered trying to blow it up at one point. Our beloved friends had been spying on us the whole time, but saved their applause until the end.

Bret had proposed marriage on the night we lost our v-cards to each other, of course he forgot the next day, but here we were over a decade later and he was about to make the same proposal. "If we're not married when we're forty we should marry each other," he said.

The proposal, again, came from a good-hearted place. It just didn't come from the right guy.

"Oh, Bret, you're too good for me. You've always been too good for me," I said to my friend, letting him down easy, then giving him a peck on the cheek.

He inhaled his cigarette and jokingly retorted, "I know that, I just don't want to see you turn into a cat lady."

We laughed for a minute, and then I glanced over at Shay. She and Eric were intertwined and caught up in each other's spell. I recognized a love that would go the distance when I saw one. I started planning her wedding silently to myself. She couldn't have my red flowers, but I might lend her the bun.

Eventually, we made our way to our local Denny's and stuffed our faces with anything from eggs and hash browns, to mozzarella sticks and salads. We cracked jokes about our friend Robby's haircut, and the girls argued about who was the better singer. As the night came to a close, I appreciated the friendships that I knew would also stand the test of time.

Bret smiled at me knowingly. He knew our history was untouchable, but he also knew there was no room for a relationship in the future. It was one of those cases of outgrowing each other.

That night I slept at Shay's house, and we talked until the sun came up. Cuddled up together like school girls, she told me about her undying love for Eric. I told her life was short and she needed to go for it before she no longer had the option. We steered clear of any direct mention of Lloyd or my mother, I was in town for closure and a fresh beginning. We finished by thanking each other for everything and making plans for my return. We had a very special friendship. Lloyd had always called us Thelma and Louise, and it sort of stuck.

"Good night, Thelma," I said.

"Good night, Louise," she responded, and we finally got my sleep although it was already five in the morning.

I woke up around noon feeling refreshed. Well, hung over and nauseous, but definitely in good spirits. Shay and I said our see you laters, and then I was on the road to get my father and son.

When I arrived at my brother's house, Renz was impatiently waiting for me on the porch. He loved his cousins, but he and his father had plans to go fishing. I couldn't picture Marc with a fishing pole. I couldn't really picture him with anything constructive, but I was glad he was making the effort with our son.

On the car ride back, my father kept telling us these horrible jokes. I was glad to see him in good spirits, but at one point I was playing a mental radio in my head to tune him out. I listened to Renz's fake laughter as a cue for my own. Lloyd and I had an ongoing joke about fake laughter, and we'd often practice some out on each other. I started wondering if I'd ever stop hearing his laughter. What if one day I couldn't hear him anymore? I didn't see that happening, but the thought bothered me. I started to get butterflies as I pictured myself back in New York to say goodbye to the city and goodbye to him. What if I didn't get the closure that visited my mother's grave gave me when I tracked down his burial site?

I needed to feel his presence. If I could just feel him nearby, I could get my closure. I wondered how his daughter was. I wondered if the toddler knew what an amazing father she had. Of course she did, I figured. Anyone that came across Lloyd knew how amazing he was. Whether you knew him for twenty years, or you knew him because you were the cashier at the Starbucks he frequented, you felt honored to be in his presence.

I started wondering what his daughter looked like. I wondered if she had Lloyd's single dimple that would appear above his right cheek only if he laughed really hard. I wondered if she had his smile. My heart sank at the idea of losing a parent so young. I peered into the rearview window at my son. I was so thankful for what I did have, what Renz had, what we had together. The past few years were traumatic, but I was very lucky to see another day.

As we approached my father's home, my son expressed his excitement about going fishing with his father. I still couldn't grasp the idea of Marc hooking bait. Now eating the bait, I could imagine.

After freshening up at my dad's, I was off to drop Renz off with Marc. Afterwards, I planned on going back to dad's to do some detective work to find out where Lloyd had been buried. But I was caught off guard when Marc suggested that I join the boys on their fishing venture. Fishing and golf were very big in my family. I thought Marc could probably use the assistance. Marc and I were not at all fond of each other, so I thought it might be good for Renz to see us interacting civilly for his sake.

My gut told me to concede, so I put off looking into Lloyd until the next day. To my surprise, Marc broke out a fishing kit for me. He was really taking this seriously for Renz. As he packed up his uncle's truck, Renz and I opted to get something edible for ourselves. We took off in my rental to the local deli and stocked up on sandwiches for everyone.

"I'm really happy you're coming, Ma."

My heart melted at the high pitch in Renz's voice. The understanding between Lloyd and me about children coming first was ever prevalent.

We made it back to Marc's house and all gathered into Uncle Buster's truck. I felt a little overdressed in my skin tight jumper, but at least I was wearing flats. Renz and I sat in the backseat while Uncle Buster drove and Marc took shotgun.

Renz snatched his father's cap off of him and put it on his own head. Marc retorted jokingly, "Boy, I'm gonna kick your butt."

Renz replied, "I couldn't help it. It looks better on me anyway."

I loved seeing them have these moments. Although seemingly inconsequential, I knew these small moments were the foundation of a good father-son relationship. For so long, I thought Renz would only see his father as a pair of sunglasses or a baseball cap. It broke my heart when Renz was a toddler and would go around saying "Dada" to any man he saw in baggy jeans and a baseball cap. That was the only point of reference he had for a father back then. I was so appreciative that Marc was truly making an effort to earn the title of Dad, especially when things went south with Lloyd.

Lloyd had been the only real father figure Renz had when he was younger. After we split up, I was afraid of the effect it would have on my son. I had suspicions though that they kept in contact for at least a year after our breakup. Gifts would often be sent anonymously to my parents' house for Renz. I knew who they were from, but I told Renz that they were from his dad. I told Marc to just go along with it, and being the jerk that he was, he had no problem taking credit for things he believed I had bought for Renz. By that time, Marc had started actually making some of his child support payments and he was coming around more to spend time with Renz. He even showed up to Renz's sporting events and school activities.

I was glad Renz had Lloyd when he did, but they needed to, in a sense, breakup as well. The longer they kept in touch, the harder it would be for Renz when he realized Lloyd had started his own family and had to change his priorities. Plus, I wanted to make sure Renz had a good relationship with someone, who for all intents and purposes, he was stuck with, so to speak. I wanted Renz's admiration for his father to grow in the hopes that Marc's maturity would grow as well. In that car ride to the pier, I saw the huge transformation that had taken place.

We pulled up to a pier just three miles from the beach. It was the same pier my deceased grandfather would take me to go fishing, and the same pier I spent many high school nights hanging out at. It brought back so many memories, and I was glad to share somewhat of a tradition with my son. As the men opened and placed the foldout chairs, I grabbed the cooler and food. The men got out the poles and Buster began to show Renz (and Marc) how to place the bait on the hook. I immediately grabbed a Heineken because I knew it'd be a long afternoon.

A short buzz later, I pulled my son aside to tell him about going to Los Angeles. Gwen had said that's where she heard he'd moved to and it's the last place his book put him, so I figured he would be buried there.

"So, before we make the move back to Florida, I need to go visit a friend in Los Angeles. I'm just going to go for a few days, then I'll fly back to New York and get the ball rolling with moving out of our place before heading back here to get you enrolled in school and everything," I told him.

"Ma, are you going to see Lloyd?"

I couldn't believe the question that had just come out of his mouth. He couldn't possibly know, could he?

"Why would you say that?"

"Don't be mad, but he sent me a postcard from LA a few years ago. We were kind of still talking for a while after you guys broke up. But I haven't talked to him in a long time. I swear."

"It's ok. I'm not mad," I said, relieved that he didn't know the truth. A boy could only take so much heartache and his grandmother's death had already stripped him of too much of his innocence. I couldn't tell him about Lloyd's passing. We had just gotten through the burial visit, and he was so happy in this moment with his dad. I couldn't shock him with this harsh reality, at least not right now. "Yes, I'm going to see Lloyd. I'm going to say my final goodbye and get closure."

It wasn't a lie. I was going to say goodbye.

"Tell him I miss him and that he can call me someday. I'll still be his friend. I mean, if that's ok with you."

It took everything I had to hold back my tears. I just smiled and nodded.

Thankfully, Buster and Marc started hollering, so we turned around to see what the fuss was all about. It seemed that Marc had a bite. We rushed over assuming from Marc's body language that whatever was on his line was huge. He gripped his pole as if the twister that lifted Dorothy's house was upon us. He fought that fish with all of his strength and finally reeled it in. It was a tire.

Renz and I busted out laughing as Marc's excited expression collapsed.

"Dad, it's just a tire." My son was great at pointing out the obvious.

I couldn't pull myself together. I started imitating the scene that we'd just witnessed and Renz followed suit. Even Uncle Buster was cracking up.

Typical Marc started making up excuses and blaming everything that started with a letter. He even said there was a fish and that he felt it let go at one point, but the tire hooked on after and he couldn't decipher between the two. Renz and I exchanged a look as neither of us was buying this story. Marc pouted a bit more before going off a little further down the pier to continue fishing without hearing our ridicule. He returned shortly after to prove himself with the minnow he'd caught.

I had no such luck as far as fishing went. I did, however, teach Renz how to cast and he did a great job. He caught four decent-sized fish that afternoon. Since my son was hogging up all the sea creatures, I worked on my tan. It was, overall, a good day, and I was just happy Marc and I didn't throw each other over the pier.

As the sun began to set, we made our way back to Marc's house. I kissed my son goodbye and watched him run into the house to show his dad's mother the fish he caught. Standing there, I felt overwhelmingly proud of my son. Marc, who was still unpacking the truck, looked over at me. I felt his eyes examining me.

"Don't even think about it," I said.

"What? Don't you want to stay the night?" he asked.

Then, he laughed his trademark laugh, and I told him no thanks. A few witty retorts later, I was in my rental car headed back to my dad's to wash the fish smell away.

When I pulled into the driveway, I sat there for a few moments, taking in the house. I suffered silently for years from the fact that my father and I weren't close. It was time to change that. I only wished I would have made the effort prior to my mother's passing. I went inside and there he sat in his favorite recliner watching a special on The Beatles.

My eyes filled up immediately. I thought about how many years we spent just coexisting rather than actually taking a part in each other's lives. For many years, I would barely speak to him. I wouldn't even make eye contact. Everything was so half-hearted between us. He looked over at me and asked what was wrong. I let it all out. I literally went from the age of four, to nine, to sixteen. I told him every little thing that had ever happened between us that affected me more than he ever understood. He broke down as well. We both cried, we laughed, and we argued a little. We got it all out. We had what Lloyd once called the checkmate of conversations.

The checkmate of conversation was a dialogue between two people that would change the game forever. Whether it terminated a relationship or strengthened it, it was a chance you were willing to take to end the games that we often play in life. Most people, like me, are stubborn and don't want to appear vulnerable. What Lloyd once taught me was that if you love someone enough, you will risk it all. Win or lose, you will put it all out there and possibly get to start over. I felt like Lloyd and I never had that opportunity. I felt like our checkmate conversation occurred through his book.

He finally put it all out there, but the chance to start over wasn't an option for us.

That night I told my father all about Lloyd. Even though he could not take the place of my mother, I needed a parent to spill my guts to and to set me straight. Renz was still too young to be that person for me, so my father got an ear full that night. We talked for hours on end, and he said I was doing the right thing by going to Los Angeles for closure. He also told me that a letter had come awhile back from a Lloyd, but all that was in it was a business card to a bookstore so he threw it out, thinking it was just an advertising mailer.

After our long conversation, I kissed my father goodnight and felt as though a weight had been lifted off my shoulders. I got online and booked a flight to LA and found a hotel. I figured that once I got there, I could search the county public records for death certificates and check newspaper clippings at the library for obituaries and find out where he was buried.

That night, I had my recurring dream. It was the same scene as always - a spot on the beach where the clouds met the ocean. Every color of the rainbow descended into the horizon, but the orange and yellow schemata was stronger than the rest as it sort of intertwined through every other color. I stood in front of this breathtaking image and felt the waves crash simultaneously with the pattern of my breathing. Maybe this dream was a sign that peace was on the horizon.

CHAPTER ELEVEN

L.A. Dreaming

I woke up the next morning mentally prepared for my trip. But I smelled something burning and ran to the bathroom to see if I had left the straightener on. Granted, I hadn't used the straightener or even unpacked it, but it was a habit my mother had started me on of tirelessly checking and rechecking outlets. I was relieved that I hadn't started a fire, but I still didn't know where the smell was coming from. I made my way down the stairs in a slumber-like trance, and there stood my father. I laughed and teared up at the same time when I discovered he was preparing me pancakes. Burnt pancakes, but he cooked for me nonetheless. I hugged my father and thanked him. I told him I loved him, and I meant it with all of my heart.

As I chiseled off the hard pieces of my pancakes, I drowned the rest in syrup to show him that his efforts would not go to waste. After a few bites, my father started laughing and said I didn't have to indulge him anymore. He took our plates, emptied them in the trash and said he would treat at Denny's as soon as I got dressed.

After breakfast, I started to get nervous about my trip and wanted to hear Renz's voice. Marc answered the phone when I called.

"I knew you couldn't stay away," he chuckled.

"Ew. I'd rather watch paint dry than spend any more time

with you than I had to. Stop kidding around and put my son on the phone."

"Hey, Ma."

"Hey, baby, I'm about to go catch my flight. You be good and I'll see you in a few days. Remember, Pop is around if you need anything."

My father dropped me off at the airport. Before I got out of the car, he asked if I was sure I didn't want him to join me. I had thought about bringing a companion along, but I knew it was something I had to do alone. I remembered the excitement that used to fill my soul upon traveling to see Lloyd. This trip would be so different, so empty. I kissed my father's cheek and headed for the terminal.

I put on my headphones and started listening to music as a way to distract myself from the long flight ahead, but every song brought back memories. Keith Sweat's "Nobody" came on and it brought my back to a business trip Lloyd took me on to Arkansas of all places.

As you can imagine, Arkansas wasn't exactly hopping with things to do and Lloyd ended up being busier than he'd expected because the CEO of his company had decided to fly in and hold a bunch of meetings while they were promoting a new clothing line. I had not expected to be stuck in the hotel for most of the trip while Lloyd gallivanted around with a couple models to photo shoots in barns and whatnot.

I was already on edge and a little testy, and to top things off, one of the models kept giving me side eye any time I met up with Lloyd to grab a bite to eat and just hang out when he had free time. I could tell by the way she'd smirk at Lloyd that she wanted his dick and was not pleased that he'd brought his girlfriend on location. I mentioned it to Lloyd, but he insisted that it was all in my head.

One afternoon, I was making my way to the elevator bank, and she was already waiting for one. I smiled at her in an attempt to see Lloyd's perspective. Maybe I was just imagining shit. However, she looked away as if she was too good to acknowledge me.

"Is there an issue I'm not aware of?" I said.

"Of course you're unaware," she said in the most stuck up tone.

The first thought that went through my head was that Lloyd had me thinking I was crazy when I was spot on. The next thought was that this bitch needed to have her ass handed to her.

Just as I was about to get in her face, the elevator opened and the CEO of Lloyd's company was inside. Keeping it classy, I turned around and marched right back to my room. Then, I threw all of Lloyd's clothes in the bath tub and turned the water on. It was long after that he returned to our room.

"Babe? Where are you?"

"Don't you 'babe' me. I knew something was up with that snooty model. Why'd you stick up for her? Is there something going on between the two of you?" I yelled although I didn't really think that Lloyd was cheating. I had to take my anger out on someone.

"Of course not. I just didn't want there to be drama," he said.

"Well, drama's what you got," I said and gestured to the bathroom.

I heard him start laughing, which upset me more that he wasn't taking me seriously. I ignored him and his advances for the rest of the day.

When it got late, he knew what to say to get my attention. "You have to eat, ya know. Can you stand me long enough to grab dinner?" he teased.

He had me at eat, but I wasn't ready to let him off the hook just yet. I agreed to join him for dinner, but made it clear it was only to fuel my body.

I went into the bathroom to put on my makeup and noticed that at some point, I guess during my twenty-minute nap, Lloyd must have taken his clothes to the laundry room. I giggled to myself and started putting on some lip gloss. Lloyd came up behind me and kissed my cheek. My games were wearing on me, and I wanted to stop being stubborn, but he had to first acknowledge that this was serious. His line of work called for him to be around models and beautiful people all the time, and he had to know that he had to put his foot down and let them know he was off limits. Ignoring their flirtations instead of putting a stop to them was sending the wrong signals. That chick really thought she had a shot and had the nerve to be upset by my presence.

When we got to the restaurant, I noticed a microphone and projector near the bar. It was karaoke night, which secretly excited me. I loved karaoke. But unfortunately, I also noticed the bitch, who was sitting with some other models and some of Lloyd's coworkers.

My stomach turned, and I grew nervous, worrying that Lloyd

intended for us to sit with them. Lloyd saw my uneasiness and pulled me close. He asked the hostess for a table on the other side of the restaurant.

We were escorted to our table and handed two gold rimmed menus. When the waiter appeared with a pitcher of ice water, I quickly uttered, "Martini."

I glanced over at the bitch and noticed her cocky attitude wearing off. She knew her place as she sat sipping on her house vodka.

Ten minutes passed, and it felt like an eternity. My mood wasn't improving with the swigs of my drink. Lloyd stood up, and I grabbed his forearm.

"Where are you going?" I didn't want him speaking to the girl in front of me other than the generic hi he fed the table when we walked in. He said to relax and that he was just going to the bathroom. I took a deep breath in and released his arm. It didn't even register that he walked over to the DJ rather than to the bathroom. I was so preoccupied with the table of models that were glaring at me.

All of a sudden, a familiar beat came on. I looked up to see Lloyd holding a microphone and almost choked on my blue cheese-stuffed olive. He started singing his rendition of "Nobody" while pointing to me. I threw back my third martini and looked on in amusement. He was belting out the lyrics. I had no idea what a powerhouse he was. I felt the corners of my mouth rise up and my face turned beat red. I was so proud. This was the gesture. I turned over toward the bitch with an abundance of confidence. She looked pissed. I loved every moment of it.

Lloyd knew exactly what I needed, exactly when I needed it. It's like our minds were in sync with one another. He always put me first and always made me feel like number one. His loyalty and efforts to make sure I never looked or felt stupid never ceased to amaze me. It was exactly what I yearned for in that moment.

♟♙

The next song I heard was "In My Life" by The Beatles. This song reminded me of my family. I thought for sure it was a sign from above. Maybe my mother was guiding me this whole trip. It may be farfetched to some people, but for me it made perfect sense.

The song also started me thinking about falling in love again. It was so hard to imagine someone other than Lloyd. Who could possibly fill those shoes? He was an eleven and a half after all. What happens to people that find love again after loss? If a widow remarries, who does she choose to spend eternity with - husband one or husband two? These were the thoughts that paralyzed me, yet they were the same thoughts that encouraged my belief in reincarnation.

I believed that your soul mate was the one person that you encountered in every life. Maybe each life was different and your time was spent serving a different purpose for that person. In one life you may be there to get a message to that person, in another you may be being punished for something you did in a previous life and sharing a cell with that somebody. Maybe each life wasn't designed to find love but to learn a lesson and evolve as a person. However, a soul mate would be so significant they would exist beyond the restraints of this world. As my imagination ran wild, I grew calm with the idea of eternity.

♟♟

Then the SWV song "Rain" started playing. In the beginning of our relationship, I told Lloyd my utmost fantasy was to have sex in the rain.

It was probably my second time seeing Lloyd after Daytona. He was in Georgia for work, and we both hopped in our cars on a whim and met halfway between his work site and my home at a random Comfort Inn for the night. Something was premeditated in the stars that night because shortly after he arrived, I did too to find him waiting in the motel parking lot. Moments after I stepped out of my car, rain started falling from the sky. We had already spoken about our deepest fantasies and when the rain fell down we immediately started to laugh.

We didn't even hesitate. We jumped in his car and took off to find a quiet back road. After parking behind a vacant mini mall that had been for lease, we jumped out of the car in a fit of passion. With rain pouring down our eager bodies, we began ripping each other's clothes off. My hair was cold against my bare back, and goosebumps riddled my body. Lloyd picked me up and placed me on the hood of his car. He brushed my cheek with his hand as he looked at me like I was the most beautiful girl in the world.

The moonlight cast the only light upon our faces, and everything else was pitch-black. We could only make out each other's highlighted faces, so we searched one another's body like braille. My heart was pounding almost as loudly as the raindrops that hit the pavement. Moments after, he entered my body, and a flash of lightning illuminated the scene. It was probably the most intense sexual experience of my life. The experiences Lloyd and I shared were so fateful, you couldn't make this stuff up.

♟

I sighed at the memory but was relieved that boarding had started. I was even more relieved when the anxiety-ridden flight finally touched down in California. I got in a cab to my hotel.

There was a Starbucks in the hotel so I grabbed a coffee and took a seat to collect my thoughts while waiting for it to be check-in time. Suddenly, an older gentleman took a seat in front of me. I looked at the empty tables around me as if to say take your pick buddy, but he didn't budge. The man had a lengthy grayish white beard, and he sported a skull cap. Normally, I would grow fearful, but I had endured so much shock over the past couple years that nothing could surprise me at this point. I was in a new place so of course it would be my luck for this old homeless-looking man to skin me and sell my flesh on the corner. I planned on just handing over my purse, but as I reached for my Michael Kors bag, the stranger spoke.

"How are you?"

I made sure to identify my mace inside of my bag before engaging in conversation. "I'm fine," I said politely. Maybe this man really was homeless and just wanted some change, or maybe he was a widower and was just yearning for someone to talk to.

"You are a beautiful woman."

Okay, clearly, I assumed too soon. He just wanted to get in my pants.

"Look, buddy, I'm married." I went to gather my things to leave.

"Wait a minute. I'm not coming onto you. Hasn't anyone ever given you a compliment without wanting something in return?"

The way he said that had me pondering the question.

He continued, "I was just wondering if you were as happy as you are beautiful. I know in my life all I ever really wanted was happiness. Not fame or fortune, not worldly possessions or things for vanity. Just painstaking happiness."

As he spoke, I was intrigued. My intuition told me to listen and not be afraid of this stranger.

"I wanted to be so blue in the face with happiness that people would want to punch me in the face because they got sick of my constant smiling and radiating happiness that seeped out of my being," he said and I laughed at his interpretation. "We play such a small role in the universe. We're a fraction of a fraction. For us to truly exist, to truly be living, we would have to exist in someone else's eyes. We would have to play the role of the most significant being to them."

I smiled wholeheartedly and asked, "Well, are you happy?"

He said that he was. He said after the loss of his wife and daughter in a car crash, he was able to continue in life with the same happiness because of the notion that this type of happiness did exist. He also said he felt sorry for the people that went their whole lives not knowing that type of happiness or unconditional love. I smiled again and agreed with him on that point.

"Well then, young lady, your life is fulfilled. Consider yourself lucky."

I shook the man's hand and headed out the door. I looked back at his smiling face and waved. I was ready to finish my journey.

I did think about that man a lot. I'd like to say something freaky happened, like the man was an illusion or an angel. Truth is, he was just a man with a lot of wisdom. Although he may not have been mystical or magical, he still served a purpose in finding me that afternoon. Nothing happens by chance. I felt a little braver and a little more able to face the future with the message he'd relayed.

I checked myself in and headed up to my room. As the light on the lock flashed green, I ushered my way in. The room was beautiful. It was small, but the view was exceptional. I spread my curtains as far as they could go and could see the Hollywood sign.

I took a seat on the comfy bed with my laptop. But before I could start the investigation into Lloyd's final whereabouts, I wanted to see where he lived during his final months. I would see the sights that I thought Lloyd would have loved. We were pretty attuned to each other, so I was sure I could pick out locales Lloyd would have ventured to. Maybe I would end up standing in the same spots he once had and feel his presence. This trip couldn't just be all about finding a grave. The final end to my and Lloyd's story in this life deserved more of a grand bon voyage than a sad, morbid cemetery visit. I would honor him in that way.

I freshened up in the bathroom. The revelations of Lloyd's book played over and over in my mind. I splashed some cold water on my face and gave myself one last look. Then, I headed out.

A closer look at the Hollywood sign, a visit to the Griffith Observatory, a stroll along the Hollywood Walk of Fame, a few pictures at Grauman's Chinese Theatre and my first day in Los Angeles was coming to an end. I felt I did Lloyd proud.

The next day, I devoted to going to the Santa Monica pier. Lloyd and I had discussed coming here one day but that trip never happened. But the beach, I felt, was where I would really say goodbye to Lloyd. No cemetery could hold his essence. Lloyd's soul would be at the beach. As I neared the pier and could see the iconic Ferris wheel, I hesitated. Lloyd and I had said goodbye to each other so many times, but it never had finality. I took a deep breath in and headed down to the milky white sand. I watched my footprints in the sand and admired the grains that tickled my toes.

The sun began to set, and I made my way to the shore line. As I neared the water, I felt the sand change from grainy to damp and I watched as the waves covered my feet. I looked up to the horizon and the soft breeze glided across my face. The wind blew across my sundress and swept the bob I had recently been sporting across the back of my neck. The moment was surreal, and I froze up at the vision in front of me.

It was my dream. Every color in the rainbow emerged before me. The oranges and yellows intertwined with all the other colors, and the water mirrored the sky perfectly. You couldn't tell where the horizon ended. I couldn't believe that I was seeing the exact color scheme I had always dreamt about. It was breathtaking. As my hair blew across my forehead I didn't dare use my hands to brush it away. I didn't want my hand to get in the way of my immaculate view. My heartbeats synchronized with the breaking of the waves. This was my heaven on Earth.

I started to tremble as I felt Lloyd's overwhelming presence. We had this telepathic way about us. We could always sense it when the other person would enter a room. I could feel him now more than ever.

I turned my head slowly to get the full panoramic view of my dream realized. In the distance I saw a man. As he got closer, he began to bear a striking resemblance to Lloyd. I felt my chest collapse and then inflate with air. I could now see the scar above his lip from when a dog bit him when he was eight years old. I could see the black diamond earrings I had gotten him years back. I saw his left eyebrow raised slightly higher than his right, his default expression when something surprised him. Could it really be him? The trademark qualities were all accounted for, but I couldn't convince myself this was more than a mirage or wishful thinking until he stood before me, reaching his hand to my cheek, and I could see the tattoo on his wrist. Our tattoo. My jaw dropped in astonishment. It was him. But how?

He was by far the most beautiful sight I had ever seen. He was barefoot with white pants and a black button-up shirt. His top buttons were undone which used to annoy me, but now hypnotized me. His eyes pierced through mine, and it was as if he could see into my soul. I could hear the rhythm of his heart. The sunset that haunted my dreams was not my heaven, I thought to myself. Lloyd was my heaven.

He pulled a chain from around his neck and unclasped it, letting a ring fall into his palm.

"I told myself that if I ever saw you again, I wouldn't hesitate. I would make you mine forever," he said, holding the ring up and gesturing to my left hand.

I gave it to him without question, and he slid the ring on. Neither of us had to say it. We knew what it meant. Then, it hit me.

If people could write their own happy endings, then nothing would ever end – there'd be no divorce, no conflict, no death, and, more importantly, no make-ups or second loves, I remembered him telling me once. Of course, any book written by this man wouldn't just let the characters go off to live happily ever after. Perfection was boring, he had noted. For Lloyd and Leann to have a chance, Ace had to die and put an end to that storyline. It was the only way to make room for our second chance at love, our real-life happy ending.

I noticed a woman approaching us from behind. As she neared, I recognized that it was Lloyd's aunt. She was carrying a toddler and let her down so she could run to Lloyd. I was hesitant, but made my way to them both. Lloyd and I looked at each other, tears in both of our eyes. The love was seeping out of us both. I acknowledged his beautiful daughter and noticed a pendant around her neck. It was a pink ribbon, the international symbol for breast cancer awareness. Inscribed on it was "RIP Mommy." It all made sense now.

Acknowledgments

Thank you God for giving me the gift of literature and for instilling in me the passion it takes to make a piece of literature come to life. Through him all things are possible.

Thank you to my mother for being my biggest fan, for believing in me, and supporting me through all of life's challenges. She encouraged me to never give up on my passion and was the first person to ever read my work. She was a fan of Checkmate, even before it was written. I owe my success to her unconditional love and support.

Thank you to my son, the greatest gift that life has given me. One look into his eyes was all it took for me to be driven to succeed. He is the sole purpose behind my motivation. A mother's love for her child promotes strength to conquer anything.

I would like to thank my publisher, Jasmin Hudson, for taking the time to invest in my story and for seeing something special in my work. I appreciated her hard work and dedication in bringing my story to life. I also appreciate the tireless work of the interns that have been a part of this production.

Lastly, I want to thank the man whom this story was based on. He taught me many things and awoken my spirit. He has had a huge impact on my life and, in many ways, he brought me back to life.

About The Author

Danielle Bolcar was born in Passaic, New Jersey, into a Catholic Italian family. At the age of four, her parents ventured away from the familiarity of their hometown, leaving behind quite a large extended family, to advance their careers for the sake of Danielle and her older brother. Over the years, Danielle witnessed courageous, selfless acts from her parents that inspired her to strive to one day do great things as well.

By the time Danielle reached the fourth grade, she knew her desire to write was more than just a hobby; it was a gift. An essay she wrote was published in the local paper, and the feedback she received from readers encouraged her to further pursue this newly unveiled talent. As she grew older, she fine-tuned this talent through poetry and blogs, but in her mid-twenties put her writing aspirations on hold as she became a mother and looked to other endeavors.

Danielle holds a bachelor's degree in psychology from the University of South Florida. It was not until she finished college that she decided to write her first novel. Becoming a mother inspired her to take risks and allow herself to be vulnerable to the world as she told her story.

Danielle's child taught her that with love and acceptance come disappointments and heartaches, but you cannot truly appreciate the good without the experience of the bad. This allowed Danielle the strength to produce a book with hopes for the former. Upon completing her book, she stumbled across Pen & Pad Publishing, and the rest is history.

Danielle is currently writing another novel and still resides on the east coast of Florida. She plans to see her dreams of becoming a well-known author through and looks forward to entertaining audiences from all over.

Danielle can be reached through her Facebook page: www.facebook.com/AuthorDanielleBolcar

Note From The Publisher

Dear Reader,

Thank you for buying Checkmate by Danielle Bolcar. I hope you enjoyed it.

As a small independent press, Pen & Pad Publishing does not have the luxury of a huge marketing department or the exposure of being on bookshelves across the country. If you enjoyed the book, please help spread the word and support this and future titles from Danielle Bolcar by writing a review on Amazon or telling a few friends about the book.

Also, check out other Pen & Pad books by visiting our website:
http://www.penpadpublishing.com

While on the site, be sure to join the mailing list if you'd like to hear about new releases, book signings and events Pen & Pad authors will attend.

Thanks again,

Jasmin Hudson
Owner, Pen & Pad Publishing LLC

Pen & Pad Publishing LLC
jasmin@penpadpublishing.com   /PenPadPublishingLLC
http://www.penpadpublishing.com   /penpadpublish

.

CPSIA information can be obtained at www.ICGtesting.com
Printed in the USA
LVOW11s0404190216

475805LV00001B/37/P